Johnny Egan

Goes

To War

Johnny Egan Goes to War

As told by

John David Young

To

Teresa Whitehawk

Published 2020 By EagleBear Press

In conjunction with KDP Publishing

Available on Amazon Books or by sending a request
to whitehawkt@outlook.com

Authors Note

Almost every generation of Americans have lived with the existence of war in their lifetime. The Viet Nam War was my generation's nightmare. Whether or not we had a loved one as a soldier or other military agent in the war, the Viet Nam War affected our lives drastically. The news reported it daily. Images were imprinted on our minds. The protests seemed to involve all of us as if we were there.

This is one more personal telling of those events. Even though it has been fictionalized, every war incident in this book actually happened. Many pieces have been left untold. One fact not made clear to the reader is that as a Sergeant, Johnny at age eighteen and nineteen led a platoon of fourteen men in their skirmishes and only three of them (including the teller, John David Young) survived. This telling also does not show the emotional scars worn internally that causes cynicism to be engraved in a man's soul. It does not adequately describe the recurrent and overwhelming fear that dominated that time in war. It does not show the fact that PTSD does not disappear but continues to plaque many veterans as it morphs into different forms. It may cause one man to turn to silence more often than is healthy, and another the inability to sit quietly and relax. It creates an urgent need to be moving, working, doing something, to keep the sounds, emotions and scenes of war at bay. Even the ability to hear is invaded by blank moments, as though it is the silence that happens after a bomb blast.

This telling by the veteran John David Young, is fictionalized when he talks about his life after the war. Yes, he is a musician and did have a great deal of success in the music world, but his account of family life is fictionalized to maintain his privacy. All of his memories of the Vietnam War are true. In the editing process it was my main focus to preserve his true voice.

Because of his strength of mind and purpose, some aspects of the effects of the war on his person have been left out. That he still suffers from PTSD is true, that memories surface in dreams or when he is watching the news, or a sound or event happens, then he is back in the place where those memories began. He hides the tears that surface from the pain.

Each man having gone through war is subject to diseases they would not have had in peace time. They cannot be the same person before they were put through the ordeal of war and their belief systems are altered forever.

-   Teresa Whitehawk

Johnny Egan Goes to War

By John David Young

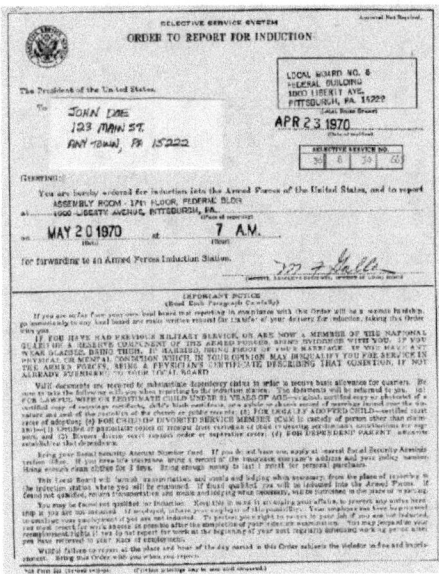

I

Graduation

The memory is as clear as looking through glass, the smile on my father's face when he handed me the letter. "Congratulations," the letter read. "Your number was selected to serve in the military, selective service #128." A little more to the point the letter explained I had ten days to report to the

Oakland processing site for induction and training. I was seventeen years and ten months old. Panic hit me. It was the height of the Viet Nam War and nine chances out of ten that is where I would end up.

"I'm enlisting," I said to my dad. The Air Force looks good."

"You'd better get to it," he said with a smile. "Don't worry. It will make a man out of you."

Right then I realized he had no idea what was going on in the world. His war, World War II, was a just and complex war, with clear beginnings and ends. He had driven a wrecker and done truck maintenance and never fired a shot in anger for his whole five years. He was billeted in England and even brought home a wife. The war in Europe was good for him. It was his mother, father, aunt and uncle and he did his duty as he was ordered and was thus rewarded.

This war was different. As president Eisenhower had said, "Beware the military industrial complex." I shuddered inside. I knew we were fighting for Oil and Money, not to mention National Military Pride.

I had been hitch-hiking often, a favorite pastime of mine in 1967. It was a way to feel free and meet strange people. It was also a bit of high adventure for a bored seventeen-year-old. I had only one goal - to become a Rock and Roll star. I had graduated early and my whole senior year had been only two classes: Mondays and Tuesdays - Problems in American Democracy and Civics.

I played guitar well and was in various garage bands, but in reality, I wanted to be in the big time, a real rocking roller. I knew I had the audacity and determination to get there. My friend Ken and I were always going to jam sessions in San Francisco. That was the place to be back then, a whole lot of garage bands. Needless to say, this draft notice put a big hitch in my plans for Stardom.

I stowed all my belongings in the grandmother cottage behind my folks' house and wondered about joining a different branch of the military, something that would fulfill my service requirement and not get my head blown off in the process. The Air Force sounded good. I had always wanted to learn to fly. I picked up the telephone and called Mel Lott, a friend of mine since grammar school. I asked him if he was still the Air Force Recruiter.

"Yep," he answered. "Got your notice, huh?"

"How'd you guess?" I asked.

"Just a hunch," he said. "Come on down to the office tomorrow. We'll talk."

My spirits were lifted! If, as I planned, I could snag a job and learn how to repair jet engines or become a pilot, I'd skip the Viet Nam thing and be square with the government too.

It was seven thirty and I was at the door of the U.S. Air Force Recruiting office to talk to Mel. He was sympathetic to my plight and willing to help.

"C'mon in" he said. He stuck his hand out to shake my hand and I got the feeling that I was in like flint. "So, you wanna be a flyboy?" he said with a laugh. Let's get started."

"We've got stiff requirements nowadays and I've got to meet them. Orders you know."

"What's step one?" I asked.

"Stand up against the wall there," he said.

I stood against the wall against a measuring tape and he backed away shaking his head and making a clucking sound in his throat.

"Can't do it Johnny!" He said with finality.

"Why not?" I asked angrily.

"You're not tall enough," he muttered.

"What?" I said loudly.

"You're not tall enough," he said, his head still shaking. "You've gotta be five foot nine – and you aren't."

"Well the damned Army will take me. Why not the Air Force?"

"Sorry Buddy," Mel said. He looked down at his well-polished shoes. "I can't ram you through against orders."

"Shit!" I exclaimed.

Mel offered, "Why don't you try Larry over at the Coastguard. Let me call him."

I sat there while he rambled on the phone to Larry for me.

He turned to me and I knew it wasn't hopeful. "No luck," he said. The Coastguard has reached their limit for the next six months. That won't do you any good. Even the CCC is full up. I think you're gonna have to bite the bullet."

I felt my heart had fallen into my shoes. It looked like that was it. I had only nine days till my inevitable doom.

Back at my folks later my dad came over and wanted to talk.

"It ain't like you're committing suicide," he started. He sat comfortably in his easy chair sipping on a beer I'd poured out for him.

"Could turn out good for you," he continued. "You've got talents they will use. Just remember this – never volunteer."

Never volunteer! I thought. That's a laugh!

That evening I told my girl-friend Karen. She was full of tears. We had a couple of good nights that I thought were awesome, then came the day I had to leave. She stood near the door of the bus and waved good-bye to me as I boarded the bus headed for Oakland. I thought she had that look in her eye that said, "I'm never going to see him again."

My leather jacket and old Levi's were heavy on me. I felt like a tiny ant being sucked up into a giant vacuum cleaner of the governmental system, never to return. My dad had said it was the adventure of a lifetime, so might as well lay back and enjoy it. He also said that life is only as good as the pleasure you can get from it. I was not having any pleasure out of it.

The bus to Oakland hummed along smoothly. The trees and rivers of the great Northwest were usually a comfort to me, but now they were just a blur. I and one small suitcase were headed for my meeting with destiny.

I laughed at myself. My girlfriend was probably already cuddling up to my friend Jerry. I knew she liked him and well, life must go on. At least for her anyway.

I drifted into a light doze and was brought awake by the sudden jerk of the bus.

The driver announced loudly, "Lunch!" we were stopped at the small town, Laytonville at the

entrance of a greasy spoon called the Red Indian
Café.

Everyone piled out and ordered the daily
special - hot turkey sandwiches. The grumble of
dialogue of other bus travelers hummed around me
like a hard wind.

Back in the bus I heard a strange voice. "Can
I sit with you?"

I looked up to see the perkiest black guy. He
was about five foot seven and very wiry. He had on a
letterman's jacket from some Oregon High School
and tight Levi's. He was also wearing sandals of some
sort.

"My name's Wilson T. Devoy," he said. "I
noticed you was alone and thought maybe you'd want
some company."

The bus jerked and he was jostled side to side.

"What the hell kind of name is Wilson T? sit
down before you fall down. My name is Johnny
Egan."

"You going to Induction too?" Wilson asked.
His voice had a bit of shakiness to it.

"Yep," I replied. "Looks like more than you
and me headed that way today. What a waste!"

"Ah no, Brother," Wilson said. "Three hots,
a cot and all the abuse you could wish for. That's the
Army."

We both laughed.

Wilson turned out to be a good friend and saw me through the nail-biting dull drums that had settled in my brain. We talked most of the way and time seemed to scoot along until we stood in San Francisco's Seventh Street Station looking for a bus to Oakland.

We ran up and down the cement of the crowded station looking for a bus to take us to Travis Air Base, our destination for induction. Finally, we found a sleepy three axel painted blue and white bus that said Travis on the side. The disinterested driver stood at the bus door and turned a smug face to us and said, "Getting Inducted?"

"Yeah," we replied. "Is this the bus we take?"

"In twenty minutes or so," he said. "You can get on now if you like. I won't wait for you. Only one bus a day, I 'spose you got a deadline to be there."

"Yeah, tomorrow," we said in unison.

He hooked his thumb and pointed over his shoulder into the bus.

We got on and waited.

An hour went by before the bus driver plonked his heavy body into the driver's seat and slowly pulled out of the terminal. I looked around and the bus was now full of scared kids all with the look of doom in their eyes. Some were loud but most of them cringed with fear. My mind was going a mile a minute trying to figure out how I could get out of this.

The bus pulled slowly into the vast expanse of Travis Field, a pit in the world where airplanes came and went. It pulled through Security, those nice upright men in uniforms doing their job. The bus stopped in front of a sign that read: INDUCTION CENTER. We all piled out and were shuffled into line by some very nice-looking women. Each of us young men were given a number, then we waited for our number to be called. It reminded me of some strange military triage.   My number was called, number 31, and I gave the lady waiting for me the letter I'd received in the mail. She looked hard at it, stamped it with some sort of verification, and pointed to another line forming in front of a barracks numbered 22.

I stood in line with the other men until one of the M.P.s directed us to Military Transport. We were told we were destined to go to Fort Ord for training - Basic they call it. I was in the Army!

II

Hijacked

We climbed out of the transport about an hour later, stiff and not at all pleased with being hijacked into the Military.

Fort Ord is a scenic place, rows and rows of barracks and M.P.s, not to mention Ordinance. There were rows of tanks and transports, guns and rifles for every visible square inch. The first order of business though, was a haircut. We were ordered into a long low hut, like a big temporary shed; and there, behind fifteen sturdy barber chairs, were fifteen serious barbers.

We all heard the order, "Pick a chair and sit in it!"

I'd always kept my hair on the short side, but in 1967 there were quite a few young men that hadn't. It was time to meet the military barbers; mostly fat bellied old-timers that saw the new recruits like meat. They seemed to have a sadistic streak in them. I remember one fellow chuckling as he took his clippers in hand as he eyed his next recruit.

I was realistic about this. I knew I was in for a buzz cut so I went with the flow. But there were others that didn't have a clue. There was this one guy next to me, an arrogant slob, that had his name on his hand carry bag. Mc Bath it read. I assumed that must have been his name, but I never found out for sure.

"Take a little off the sides and back," he said to the barber. "And be quick about it."

I turned to see the gleam in the sergeant's eye as he took the clippers to this guy's curly mane and buzzed him naked to the bone.

Mc Bath yelled and cussed at the barber sergeant until finally the barber whistled and two large M.P.s walked up and explained it to him.

"You're in the army, Son," said one. "It's regulation."

If the recruit didn't calm down it was apparent the MPs would escort him out of the chair and building.

In about an hour we all stood in another line, this time naked to the world, except for shoes, shorts and T shirts, awaiting our assignments to different D.I.'s.

What is a D.I. you ask? It is a cruel hearted man ordered to train you to survive the shit the Army is going to throw you into, a very valuable person - A Drill Instructor.

My first D.I. was sergeant George Wattleson, an Army lifer who told us what to wear and how to wear it. We had to buy our own dress uniform and were told that the Army would gladly deduct the price from our pay, but then they gave us boots and regulation battle fatigues, and that means they are either too big or too small to be comfortable.

Wattleson assigned us our bunks and taught us how to make them and strip them. Sheets and pillows were stored in a locker at the foot of each bed. The sheets were collected twice weekly by two cute civilian employees named Gladys and May. The sheets were then laundered and returned to us the same day. Your bunk had to pass the quarter test daily. What's the quarter test you ask? Well if your D.I. could bounce a quarter on it and it would flip over (because you got things tucked in tight enough) you were cool. If the quarter did not bounce the D.I. would strip your bunk and you made it over again — until the quarter flipped.

We were sent to do odd jobs, like policing up the yard — in other words, we picked up all the trash. We cleaned the toilets, and all sorts of crappy jobs with strict time limits.

Old George Wattleson must have been a veteran of the First World War. He had mellowed some. It was my second D.I. that was the corker. R.J. Baker with hash marks on his sleeve, showing he had been in the service for twenty years. He'd been everywhere and done everything and his specialty was hand to hand combat. His back was straight, his belly flat, and he was the damnedest peacock you'd ever meet.

On the first day, R.J. stood in front of about thirty boys and explained what the ward "Tenshun" meant. "You do not salute me," he said in that slow Southern drawl all the career men seemed to develop. "And do not call me sir!" he emphasized. "That is only for officers! I shall be addressed as Sergeant Baker. Is that clear?"

The boys answered in sync, "Yes, Sergeant Baker."

"I am here to teach you how <u>not</u> to get your ass kicked or killed, should you lose your weapon."

He stood eyeing the group of recruits until his eyes caught sight of a big Native kid.

"You! Number seventeen – come forward," he snapped.

The kid must have been no less than six foot six inches. He lumbered up and stood in front of R.J. Baker and all his brawn of five foot seven.

"Now, son, try to take me out."

The Native kid, Nelson I think his name was, shrugged his shoulders, doubled up his fist and swung at R.J.

R.J. ducked smoothly, and neatly swept Nelson's legs out from under him with one leg. Now

Nelson was pissed and got up and ran at R.J. Again R.J. moved swiftly, put his thumb neatly behind Nelson's ear and drove him like a falling rock down into the parade ground.

"Now git back in formation, son," R.J. said. He stood straight backed with a slight smile. "Now you know that I am not just talk, that I know my business. When you are done training with me, you will be able to do that to me. Now run!"

There is an exercise course that runs along the rim of Fort Ord that is twelve miles long. We ran it twice daily. A lot of the recruits were whooping and coughing at such treatment, but R.J. ran with us.

"Breathe!" he would say. "If it hurts, breathe!"

It was a grueling six weeks - my time with R.J. Baker, but when it was done, I was flat bellied and straight backed just like him. He would come into the barracks at three o'clock in the morning and shout, "Revilee – it's not a shock, let go of your cocks, it's three o'clock in the morning!"

Up we would jump, make our bunks, and dress. Inspection followed and then we ran.

It was only every day at 12:30 after mess that we were exposed to our weapons. We spent hours just learning how to field strip our weapon, then target practice on the range. I had a talent for guns. My dad had given me a hunting rifle when I was twelve. I took the NRA course when I was still a child and was familiar with weapons. It wasn't a great reach for me to figure out that the Army's marvelous M-16 was a piece of shit! We might as well have thrown rocks at the enemy; that would have done more damage, but here we were, each assigned an M-16.

I qualified quickly and got marksman in my first three days. R.J. was impressed. He singled me out for some reason, maybe because I was as short as he was, and taught me how to fight much bigger men.

"This will come in handy," he'd say. "Where you're going."

Well, at that point none of us knew where we were going

I qualified quickly because I thought there was no use learning how to do things unless you learned them well. How wrong I was!

We were given leave, a twenty-four hour break, and expected to be back in our bunks by 6 a.m. the next day. The local whores saw a lot of business that day. For my part I sat on a seat in Meg's Bar sipping beer. It had a rancid canned last year flavor. Well, who should show up but R.J. Baker, Staff Sergeant plus.

"Well," he said curtly. "John Egan, fancy meeting you here"

"Hello Sarge," I replied, not too happy seeing him here.

"I know that I'm the last face you want to see right now, but I got news," he said. "Tomorrow is the time our Bird Colonel comes asking for volunteers for Special Forces."

He gave me a wink. "If that ain't your aim, look small, tough, and they'll pass you by."

"Thanks, Sarge," I replied. "Nice of you to give me a heads up."

"You're a good man," R.J. said. "Don't want 'em ruining you before you even start."

He winked at me again and slid out of Meg's Bar like a retreating spirit.

I stumbled back to base and fell into my bunk and passed out, leaving tomorrow for when it arrived. Revilee came and I awoke to a sharp sunny morning full of promise - the promise of things to come that I didn't want to hear.

"Formation!" barked R.J. We were up, bunks made and standing in twos when this new god-awful man with brass Eagles on his chest came striding through our little group.

"Tenhut!" barked R.J. again. We all stood at attention.

"Fine group, Sergeant Baker, fine group!" said the Colonel.

"I'm Colonel Mc Cord," he said. He had that calmness that rank gives a man with the knowledge he can throw your ass into the brig for spitting sideways any time he chooses.

"Fine men," he said to himself. "I'm looking for volunteers today," he said slowly. "For airborne training." There were no responses. He looked up and down the crew and then he pointed.

"You. You, you, and you," he said. I thought I had skated through, but then he looked right at me and said, "And you."

I stepped forward and asked permission to speak.

"What do you want, Soldier?" the Colonel asked.

"I believe, sir," I said firmly. "That I do not fit the height and weight category for airborne, sir."

He stood directly in front of me and looked me up and down. He smiled and said, "That's odd. We need good rat-holers." He looked me in the eye and smiled, there was no chance for appeal. I was going to airborne training.

I was devastated. The shock hung over me like a large black cloud. I was to be trained at the Airborne Academy in Fort Benning, Georgia.

III

R.J. Baker

In my mind the shock was like someone had picked me to stand against a wall and be executed. 'Good Lord!' I thought. 'Those are the guys they put into the thick of things, and less than 50% of those men survive.'

R.J. came up to me, patted me on the back and said, "Congratulation Egan. Now you're one of the few. It's an honor."

"Thanks, Sarge," I replied with a feeble voice.

I got a phone call later that day. It was my girl-friend Karen. She was coming into the city (San Francisco) and wondered if we could get together. I requested a 48 hour leave and I was surprised when I got it. I hopped on a bus and pulled into the Seventh

St. Station about 5:30 in the afternoon. She was there to meet me.

"My God," she laughed. "You've got no hair!"

"Yep," I replied. "That's the way they like us, peeled and ready to boil."

We kissed and it was good. As I held her in my arms, she felt like a necessary weight to ground me. I wanted to be right there forever.

I flagged a taxi, and we went back to the room she had rented at the Saint Francis Hotel.

"I heard from your folks that you were going to be shipped off to Fort Benning," she said. "That's a long ways away." She smiled and slipped out of her clothes and walked toward me. That was the only time I've been told goodbye with sex and I knew it was the last time we would make love. She was getting rid of the last vestiges of Johnny Egan that haunted her.

It was unsaid the next morning, but I knew by the way she hurried me back to the bus that this was the end for John and Karen. I knew it wasn't right that she should wait for a guy that might not be coming back home.

I drug myself back to Ford Ord just in time to pack my duffle bag and get on another bus to Travis. There were sixteen of us that were called McCord's 'volunteers' and only one of us was happy to be going to Benning. Among those few men I was delighted to see my friend Wilson T. Devoy. He was all smiles. He planted himself in the seat next to me.

"Why Johnny," he said. "They got you too?"

"I'm a Mc Cord Volunteer," I said.

"Me too," he replied. "But I never volunteered."

I was delighted deep down into my soul that this good-natured guy was with me. It was like holding hands with someone as you prepared to be shot.

We 'volunteers' were herded off the bus and onto a military transport that ran on up to a big C 148 plane to be flown to Benning. We were all silent with anticipation of the unknown.

We flew about four hours and set down in St. Louis, changed planes and flew two more hour to Ft. Benning, Georgia. The air was thick with moisture. It was one of those sticky days they so often have there. If was steaming hot and we soon had our jackets off to shirt sleeves.

We boarded another troop transport and ended up in a village of low Quonset huts next to a sign that said, M.O.V.E. with an arrow pointing to a small hill in the distance.

"Welcome to Ft. Benning," a loud lieutenant said. "Here you will learn how to exit aircraft in parachutes, guerrilla tactics and all in all become better soldiers.

A murmur came through our group. I thought cynically to myself, 'This is going to be fun, more training, more discipline. How the hell did I get into this?'

I remembered the bus stop when we were still in California. 'If only I had taken that cute little blonde up on her offer to stay with her in Barstow. Here I am at Fort Benning.'

More exercise, live ammo courses and climbing high poles to make a jump. They ran us unmercifully. I was in such good condition that my body was hard all over. I could do 200 push-ups and never feel tired. I could do the same in sit ups. They took us to the river that flows behind the fort and we swam. We swam with full packs and weapons. We practiced hand to hand combat, and I thought of R.J. - how he taught me to takedown men bigger than me. Next, we had a huge exercise in tactics, day after day for almost another full six weeks and we were now approaching 1968.

We had two leaves while I was at Fort Benning. You could stay on the base and screw around in the nearby town, or you could take a bus into Atlanta. I decided to go to Atlanta.

It was a big, modern town, not the image of an antebellum town I had imagined it to be. If you wore your uniform you got the same cold shoulder from most of the civilians including the girls, and the only difference between the townspeople I had seen on the West coast was the Southern accent.

I felt alone and longed for the caring touch of my girlfriend Karen, but I figured she was getting what she wanted back in Eureka, my hometown.

Then I met a girl. Her name was Sandra, and she was a student at Georgia Tech. We had barely met and stood beneath a tree in the city park.

"Are you lonely soldier?" she crooned.

I was speechless. I hadn't heard a friendly female voice since my last night with Karen.

"Just a little," I replied. I could feel the foolish grin on my face.

"Are you on a 48?" she asked.

"Yep," I answered.

"Then we'd better not lose any time, she said. She kissed me deeply.

It was the best 24 hours I'd spent in six months. Those Southern girls know how to love a man. Now I was on the bus back to Benning with fond memories of Atlanta and Sandra.

Phase two of our training was jumping out of airplanes. We spent three days with a corpulent sergeant named Brogan learning how to pack parachutes.

"Your life depends on this skill," he would say. "The fall is wonderful, but it's that sudden stop at the end that's a killer." Needless to say, all of us paid close attention.

It was on a Wednesday, as I recall. We were all dressed up, full uniform, full backpack, battle gear, guns and cheerful smiles. Brogan barked orders at us and we were in a military transport headed for the airfield. We were on our way to our first real jump. Prior to this, we had spent hours zip lining off of towers. That didn't seem so bad, but today was the real thing.

We were herded onto an old C-47 and seated alphabetically. My name being Egan meant I was third, after Anderson and Butler.

"What if my chutes don't open?" I asked Sergeant Brogan.

"Then it's been an honor to serve with you," he said with his best son-of-a-bitch smile. At that moment I sat there and could see no real good reason for jumping out of that too solid airplane, but the Army saw it otherwise.

"Hook up!" Brogan ordered.

My legs felt like jello, but I would be god damned if I'd give the Army or Brogan the satisfaction of chickening out.

"You've got two rip cords on these chutes," he reminded me as he shouted over the din of the engines. "If the first one don't open, pull the second one. It's located just below your right tit. If it don't open, then God bless you."

The green light came on that signaled our move. We charged out the door, my heart rising into my mouth. I felt the rip cord pull and when my chute deployed, I said a silent prayer to the Creator. My little inner voice kept saying, "Egan, you take too many chances with your life."

I've depended on that little voice to get me out of many a scrape that I wasn't intelligent enough to avoid. It was a handy tool.

Seconds later I hit the ground and rolled, just as we had rehearsed. The buck sergeant on the ground gave me a .9 - almost a perfect score.

We all excelled I guess, so much so that they started calling us Mc Cord's Raiders from Fort Ord. I keep saying we. There was Wilson T. Devoy, Big Dick Zieback and Nico Paul Pasquine, Gary for short. We three were all part of Colonel Mc Cord's "Volunteers." They grouped us together in just about everything. There was one more man, a Native kid named Skip, but Skip got shot in a live-round exercise. As I remember, he panicked and stood right up into the line of fire. He was plugged in the shoulder and afterward was sent home. The Army didn't like damaged goods before training. So it was Willy T., Big Dick and me, with Gary bringing up the rear.

In sixty days we received our rank and a nifty little patch of a lightning bolt with the number 82nd on it. I was E3, that would be a buck Sergeant. The others were E2, or Corporals. I guess I made rank because the other guys were always asking me, "What do the hell we do?"

Gary excelled in heavier guns. He was trained in using the B.A.R. That would be the Browning Automatic Rifle. It shot 30.06 shells. The rest of us were given the miraculous M-16. It was a piece of shit. It had .223 calibers and was always jamming. They said if we cleaned it regularly it would be fine. That was among the many other lies the Army told its soldiers.

We were long armed into the 82nd Airborne as the McCord's Raiders group and were now trained. The next thing was deployment.

I got a phone call just before we were to be deployed, from none other than R.J. Baker, my first D.I. He told me the scuttlebutt was that we were to go to Germany. My heart rejoiced. That was a no shoot sort of Military Police Force for keeping the Russians at bay. Well, in about a week I and fourteen other fellows boarded a C-147 and flew over the North Pole to an American hole in Germany named Weisbaden. I and the other three thought that we'd missed the bullet and could bring home nice blond-haired wives.

Hah! Military logic!

IV

Weisbaden

We almost pranced on that plane. Our commanding officer was none other than Colonel Alan McCord, the son-of-a-bitch that volunteered us from Fort Ord. He called us "his boys," but we four 'volunteers,' hated his guts. I remembered how he flipped his fingers at me saying, "E3, good going Egan!" I saluted him at the time, but the pain I felt in doing it was extreme. His presence did not make me smile.

The plane came down out of a thick bank of clouds to Weisbaden Air Base. The lights lit up the runway like an aircraft carrier; it looked almost like fireworks.

Things were much less austere at Weisbaden. We were billeted with other men of Airborne 82nd, and things Military seemed almost civilized. It was then that McCord's Raiders got an addition – Left-hand Louie, E2 or Corporal Lewis Benson. He was another Southern boy and told the story about when he was trained by the D.I. When we marched, he always started with his right foot and the rest of us always started with the left foot. The D.I. had to place a rock in Louie's left hand so that he would know which foot to start with.

Louie was not very bright, but Jesus, could he shoot. He could put four out of five shots in the bulls eye from three hundred yards. They wanted to make him a sniper, but he didn't have the stomach for it.

Louie was a pleasant sort and fit right into our little club. The women loved him, and he wasn't on base more than twenty minutes before some girl came looking for him to take her out. Weisbaden was good in 1968, a pretty alpine city with lots of blonde babes all about twenty years old. They loved American Service Men, and most were husband hunting. Louie fit the bill.

The Military kept us busy training, up at six a.m., then a twelve-mile run, calisthenics and the rifle range. We were in top shape, ready to meet the dreaded Ruskies on a moment's notice. We spent two weeks in the loving arms of Germany; then it came.

We got orders to ship out. We were going to Viet Nam.

Command again put us on a C-147 and we flew over the North Pole back to Travis. We then were put on another C-147 and flew non-stop to Clark Field in the Philippines. We were there to acclimate. We sang the song from Country Joe and Fish (a popular band) which had a hook line of "Don't know and don't give a damn; the next stop is Viet Nam."

We were downhearted, to say the least.

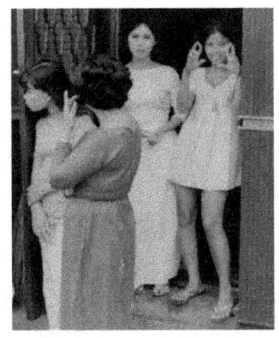

V

Clark Field and Rosie's

Clark Field lays twenty-one and two clicks kilometers away from Manila. It's a huge, smoggy city set on the lower side of the island opposite from Clark Field. We were groomed, clipped and vaccinated for every known disease. Then there were the films. We sat through the most gruesome Venereal Disease films that inspired you to never want to touch another woman – ever!

Most of the diseases that have plagued mankind took root in the Far East, because the amount of people there are so crammed together that it made contracting disease inevitable.

Clark Field was an interesting place. It was filled with every type of person you could think of. The CIA guys were the best though; their uniforms were short sleeved, with pin striped shirts, slacks, sunglasses and slicked back hair. They believed they were being "undercover." The place was crawling with them. They sat in the mess cafeteria next to the officers, acting covert and smoking expensive cigarettes. My friend Willie T. mused about them with the comment, "If we shot one, what sort of hell would break loose."

I didn't want to think about that.

Manila itself is a singular sort of place. There are all sorts of people of all ethnicities running around like rats in a cage come dinner time. Very prevalent on the Army base were young Asian women looking for a man to love and a wallet to thrive on.

And the women in town loved the G.I.s from Clark Field. At Rosie's Whorehouse they especially loved the service men. Rosie's is a tradition in Manila. It was started way back in the late 1920's and has survived Japanese and American Occupation since then. The girls are all supposed to be clean and clear of disease and working for their daily bread. HAH! One of the worst doses of clap I'd ever heard of came straight from there. The poor fellow damned near was rifted out (burst open) - it took him 28 days to get better.

Before we had heard of the man's terrible predicament, Big Dick Zieback and I were determined to experience the phenomenon of Rosie's. We had a leave and caught a troop transport into Manila and found ourselves standing right on Columbus Avenue in front of Rosie's with the bright Neon sign in pink blinking off and on.

There were some real good lookers sitting on the steps, smiling and giving us the eye. One of the girls sidled over to Big Dick and another one came over to me. We didn't say much; they knew what we were there for. We paid our $150 each to the girls and were wined and dined to all the very best of everything. Then we were escorted upstairs to a big bedroom. You had to lie down on a big brass bed and the girl you were with asked you what you liked.

"My name is Betty," both girls said in broken English. "We obey your every command."

We were jolly and having the time of our lives – full and complete. As couples we retired to separate bedrooms and from the other room, I heard Betty number 1 who was with Big Dick saying very loudly, "Oh, my god! You ain't sticking that into me!"

I could hear some tussling and some moaning and a big sigh of contentment. Big Dick didn't get his nickname for being six foot four. It was in high school gym when all the guys discovered in the dressing room that he was six inches longer than everyone else. That's when they started calling him Big Dick. An appropriate name for an average size guy with the biggest penis you'd ever seen.

When we left Rosie's, Betty number 1 was as happy as a clam, cooing and rubbing all over Big Dick like a cat.

"You come back," she shouted. "Next one be free!"

"Jeesus Big D!" I said. "You've sure got a way with the ladies!"

"Oh, shut up, Egan," he replied. "It's my magnetic charm."

We got back to base only to find there was a roll call. The Second Division was moving out to somewhere. The CIA guys were active too. I always distrusted those guys with their white shirts and dark glasses. Whenever there was a big troop movement they were there along with the Brass. But McCord's Raiders were swallowed up in the action. Big Dick and I had just barely made it for roll call, throwing on our boots and fatigues on the run. The guard at the gate didn't even look at our passes. He just jammed us through with a wide arm signal. No one could tell us where the big troop movement was going. It was all 'hush, hush, but we guessed. It was Viet Nam!

We were all assembled, waiting for orders. Then came a moment I'd never forget. The colonel came to check us out. Yes, his majesty Colonel Colin Powell. I've never seen such a rag tag collection of troops come to attention as one like that for anyone but the Colonel. He had the utmost respect of every officer and soldier. His dark skin and sunglasses, his stature and regal bearing screamed 'leader' and you could feel his critical gaze on you. He saluted us and didn't say a word. He was the one and only man each of the draftees would lay down his life for and never ask why. When he saluted the men, they all felt dismissed with honor.

VI

Viet Nam

We were fitted and loaded onto another C 147 to be delivered and distributed in Viet Nam. Each man had a helmet, helmet liner, flack vest, gun, ammo and a bad attitude. In your pack, which was a heavy old thing, you had MRE'S (Meals Ready to Eat and full of preservatives), a trench knife and shovel, six pairs of socks, two pairs of pants and T shirts and a small eating dish. With the dish the pack came to about 68 pounds. They did not distribute much ammo. You were expected to visit the Armory for that. Yes, we were all set to stand tall and fart fire for the mighty U.S.A.

It was rumored that we were to be landed at the huge Da Nang Airport, all 160 of us. We sat like dummies in the final throes of our lives!

The C – 147 is a marvelous airplane. It can carry six tanks, four jeeps and 160 troops at a time with no sweat. It is a jet and stinks like 1500 gallons of jet fuel set on fire at one time. You sit on benches with seat belts to keep you from flying around inside the jet while you're airborne, and a jolly air Lieutenant barking orders at you.

"We are bound for the airbase at Da Nang," he shouted. "There you will be distributed throughout the country as needed."

I was depressed, as far down as the laces on my boots. In my mind I kept seeing my coffin with Chevrons under my name. "Here lies sergeant John Egan."

"Fuck those people," I said to comfort myself. "They're gonna have to bring a whole division to take me down."

Those are the kinds of thought you have while in transport. The true horror and insignificance of yourself as a soldier has yet to make its way into your brain. You are one infinitesimal human raising up in the miasma of life and all you can do is keep from being consumed – if you can.

Da Nang is a coastal city, about three clicks from the South China sea. It looks all white from the air. At about six miles from the airport you can smell it. The whole place smells like an unlimed shit house. The first thought that runs through your mind is, "Jesus, do people live in this?"

As the C-147 made the approach loop I heard a voice say, "Incoming!" and then a noise like golf balls hitting the side of the aircraft assaulted my ears.

It seems we were landing in the midst of an enemy attack.

There was a bump and the C-147 veered off to the left. I could see a smoke trail of an enemy Mig crashing and burning into the City. Then all was quiet. We landed smoothly and I was glad and relieved to feel Mother Earth under my feet.

"Wahoo!" Shouted Willie T. "Did you see that? That jet of ours took him right out!"

I said sarcastically, "That was our welcoming committee."

Another soldier said, "It was the new F-16 they're trying out!"

Then another soldier's voice said, "They're Navy, based on some damned aircraft carrier out to sea. Lotta fire power."

We climbed out of the C-147 into the hustle and bustle of a war-time airport. There was no *esprit de corps* here. You lined up and another damned Lieutenant told you where to go. We were told right off that we were to go to a place called Hue Phii. We discovered it was a converted garbage dump made into a prison camp for Viet Cong.

Hue Phii, pronounced, 'Why Fee,' was our first billet in this living cesspool called Viet Nam.

We got off the Troop Transport just in time to see the ARVN, Army of Viet Nam, pushing a line of prisoners out to a different location. The prisoners were dressed in rags and most of them were barefoot in shackles.

"They must be really bad dudes," said Pasquini.

Then it happened.

A prisoner at the end of the line slipped in the mud. One of the guards kept screaming at the prisoner to get up. The prisoner had had a bad fall and struggled to get up but couldn't. He looked old and weak. The guard drew his side arm and shot the man in the head! The guard left the bloody corpse lying there while they walked double-time to get the other prisoners out of the area.

I heard Willy T. exclaim, "That son-of-a-bitch!" Then I hear him lock and load. I reached out swiftly and put my hand on his weapon. I didn't have any words for the brutality we had just witnessed, but I knew Willie T. had to control himself. We were not to intercede with the ARVN.

The blood from the fallen prisoner leaked out in a puddle around him. He was dead. There was nothing any of us could do to save him.

"I ain't fightin' for these bastards," Willie T. said to me. "You shoulda let me shoot him, Egan!"

I didn't have any flowery words to say, but I remembered my training as a sergeant and just said, "Deploy."

We set up our gear in the small buildings that had housed the prisoners. It was damp and full of huge black cockroaches. We lit one building on fire that seemed infested with them beyond control. The roaches just emptied out of that building and disappeared into the other buildings.

Most of the men erected yurts, not real yurts, but that was our slang for utility retreat shelters - two poles with a wire stretched over them and anchored to the ground, a rain tarp thrown over the small structure. The yurts seemed a better option than the cockroaches.

So here we camped out in yurts just south of Da Nang, waiting for orders. There was nothing to do but clean our weapons or eat an M.R.E., a prepared Meal Ready to Eat, and then snooze. Some corps men came and took away the dead body. The blood had already sunk into the dirt and had started to stink. The thought struck me that if there was a heaven and hell, we'd just been thrown into the latter.

In the night we were surprised by small motor bikes that came into the camp, each one carrying a small Da Nang whore. They took turns calling out to us as they wormed their way in and out of our yurts. "Blow-job! Good fuck!"

We sat up and stared at them through the semi dark.

The M.P.s just ignored them as if they were part of the landscape. One of them stopped her motor bike by me. She looked to be at least forty, but she had a ton of make-up on. She wore a sheath dress with white dragons printed all over it. She smiled alluringly and said, "Good blow-job Joe? Only $10 American." I waved her off, but she was persistent. She put the kick stand down and waddled over to me.

"Be good for you. Good for me. I like Joe's."

My mind screamed at me. "Not even with a whole-body condom!" I dug in my pocket and peeled off a ten-dollar bill from my shrinking wallet. I threw it out at her and she grabbed it before it could hit the ground. I motioned for her to go. She just grinned, got back on her motor bike and headed out of camp.

Willie T. sat up next to me. He poked his head out of his shelter and said, "You shoulda fucked her."

"Good Lord, no!" I replied. "You saw the V.D. films. I ain't being a casualty that way!"

Finally, about one a.m., the noise of the little motor bikes receded and faded away.

We spent three days in the wonderful Hue Phii, so close to Da Nang that you could hear the traffic going by. It was a busy metropolis always under fire. Both the North and South wanted to capture the city, but business seemed to go forward no matter the pressure of artillery fire. From Hue

Phii you could also look out onto the South China Sea. I noticed oil derricks some way out in the waters and American Battle Cruisers protecting them. The scream of jets was often heard in the distance.

We were herded again into Troop Transports, those big M13 things, and headed for troop dispersion in a place called La Trang. The Army-like big, armored vehicles rumbled and coughed all over South Viet Nam. As the country sped by us, we could see men and women in large woven pointed hats; they looked up at us. I'm sure they were familiar with the coming and going of the military by now. Their eyes had blank stares on expressionless faces. They looked down quickly when you caught their eyes. It was an Asian thing I learned later. They think it is rude to look one another in the eye.

The troop carrier rumbled along. Suddenly there was a big thud and a loud bang. The front end of the troop carrier collapsed into the road. There was a sound like a popcorn machine going off all around us and the cries of wounded men was echoing in what a moment before had been a serene landscape.

"Follow me," I yelled. "Lock and load!" the men tumbled out of the M13 behind me and took positions behind the road berm.

"If you see it, shoot it!" I said. There was a great deal of smoke and confusion. I saw a little Asian man carrying an RPG. I shot him and the rocket he carried discharged and blew him to bits.

Gary was close to me, busy with his B.A.R. I was shaking from the shock of the man's death and I noticed I'd pissed my pants. I was so scared my stomach was up in my mouth. My head pinged with a high ringing in my ears. There was crying and moaning, men calling for their mothers. It was out first contact with the enemy

The front end of the Troop Carrier was completely blown away. I don't think even enough of the drivers' bodies were found to make a burial. Back then we called it a road bomb, but now that kind of explosion is called an IED. Four brick shaped blocks of C4 and an impact detonator is a simple but very effective bomb.

It was quiet and the VC that had attacked us were dead to a man. I heard a Lieutenant praising me for quick thinking. "Yes, Sir," was all I could say.

"Get your men on that M13," he said. "We've got to hit Nha Trang in two hours."

That was the first painful lesson I learned about this war. No one gave a damn about anything, least of all you.

Huddled shoulder to shoulder in that dusty stinking M13, I could see the wide, frightened eyes of my guys. Left-hand Louie was crying. Big Dick fumbled for a cigarette, and Willie T. was no longer cracking jokes. His head hung in quietness and his eyes were closed.

There was nothing to say except some half-assed encouragement from me. The scene of that old man being blown up kept playing and replaying itself in my head.

"You guys did good out there," I finally said. "Hell of a way to start a vacation though."

The M13 rumbled on to Nha Trang. We were on the big Highway 1 that led down the coast. It reminded me of Highway 1 in California, except the trees were different.

I was thinking about home, how the Northwest wind left a cool spot on your skin and how it made you feel good to be alive. Here all you could smell was the stink of the South China Sea and wonder if this breath would be your last.

Welcome to Viet Nam!

VII

Nha Trang

Our M13 pulled into a high traffic section of Highway 1, then right into a huge, barbed wire and fenced compound. Lots of M.P.s and an occasional long black limousine carrying important people.

To the left there were lines of tanks and airplanes stacked as if they were ready for Christmas delivery. We were at the heart of the U.S. presence in Viet Nam. I kept waiting for the winged monkeys (enemy planes) to come up out of the sea, but I missed their gallant appearance.

"Jesus," I said to myself. "All the V.C. would have to do is set fire to this place and it'd all be over."

The troop carrier went the long way around the base to the enlisted barracks. Troop quarter # 115. Yep, that's where they put us with orders to wait.

"Why don't you smoke?" asked my friend, Big Dick Ziebak.

"It's a long story" I replied.

"Well, we sure have time," he said.

"Ok," I began. "I was five or six years old and I was my dad's shadow. He always chewed Copenhagen. I kept at him with, "I could do that." So one day he got tired of my shit and said, "Ok, son, take a pinch."

I stepped up to him, took a big three fingered pinch of chew like I'd seen him do. I stuck it between my cheek and gum like he did. But it kept working its way to the back of my mouth and I automatically swallowed it! oh, my god it was terrible – and I threw up right away. In fact, I kept throwing up until there was nothing coming up except bile. I was a very sick little boy. It took me three days to get over it. since then tobacco products have no appeal to me. In fact if I had to smoke it'd just make me start retching. So – I don't smoke.

The other men were listening and there was general laughter, left-hand Louie said in his Southern drawl, "Hell, we bit off a chew of plug before we was ten. What's the matter with you?"

I shrugged and said, "I'm just a sensitive soul."

Our jabber was cut short when a lieutenant poked his head in the barracks and said, "Ten hut!" then a colonel from the Medical arm came in. He still had his white lab coat on.

"Gentlemen," he said loudly. "You need to report to Med-branch at 14:00 for examination. "I heard you were in a firefight. We need to check you out. That is all."

The man disappeared and Willie T. asked, "Who the hell was that?"

"It don't matter" I said. "It was orders from the bird on his shoulder. I guess we'll all go up to Med."

My platoon, such as it was, 12 guys in ragged shape, made our way out onto a parade ground, got in another M13 Troop Carrier, and headed to the Med-branch. It was located half a mile from barracks 115. When we rumbled up to the Med-branch I noticed it was a hospital that looked to be taken over by the U.S. Military with large tents attached to what was once a parking lot.

"Tent number Two," said the Colonel. "Strip down to your skivvies."

I noticed there were hooks for your clothes inside the tent with each hook labeled Med 1,2, 3.

I said to my men, "Hang up your clothes here; they look unused." Soon we were twelve men standing in our shorts, waiting again for orders.

About the same time a nurse, a cute little Vietnamese girl, showed up and said, "This way boys."

We were escorted into a big tent with bright neon lights and a bunch of aides and doctors that we could hear saying to each man, "Turn your head and cough."

It all went very fast except for one man. He had a raging case of VD. He was at the table right next to me and the doctor looked at him with concern.

"It's Bullhead Clap," the doctor said. "Come right over here young man and let me look this up in my Medical reference book."

The man followed him obediently. The doctor took his huge tome out from under the table and kept coaxing the soldier to come closer. The doctor opened the book to some section and then swiftly slammed the book on this soldiers cock. Blood and pus shot out everywhere!

The soldier screamed at him, "You pig fucking son-of-a-bitch!" At the same time two nurses came up and stuck the young man with syringes full of gamma globulin. The soldier hopped around holding his genitals and swearing. Then the doctor ordered him, "Go take a piss, soldier, and don't stick that thing into anyone for at least two weeks! Dismissed!"

I cringed and said, "Poor bastard."

The doctor looked hard at me and stated in a matter of fact voice, "He had a dose of Bullhead Clap. It needed to be busted open so he could piss.

It's always tough with that stuff. Maybe he'll be more careful where he sticks that thing from now on."

He peeled off his blood-stained lab coat and put it in a hamper labeled 'infectious.' Then he turned on his heel for the next case.

To say that I was amazed was an understatement. I resolved right then that I would not touch a single lady as long as I was in Viet Nam. I heard that poor soldier in the latrine later on. He was in so much pain that he bent the pipes over his head that fed the basin.

After the physicals we were ordered to assemble at barracks 115 for deployment. It seemed that Mc Cord's Raiders were to be used for LRP, short for Long Range Patrol. Our orders were short, "Get the damned Green Berets out of trouble they have stirred up." It was a wonderful job.

We were ordered up to Corps 1 – a place called Firebase Six. One place or another in this god-forsaken country seemed all the same to me. I was wrong. Some places were worse than god forsaken.

That night I slept in a curled up tight position, tossing and turning. The little man I had shot two days before kept replaying in my mind. Seeing the RPG blow him into little swamp bits would not fade or go away. It was a recurring dream that offended all my sensibilities.

Reveille sounded and all the troops were instantly at it, dressing for the day, making their bunks and checking weapons. A lieutenant named Martins was put in charge of us.

"Egan!" he shouted.

"Yes, Sir!" I replied.

"Get your crew over to L.S. (Landing Zone) 22. You are bound for Firebase 6!"

We grabbed our gear and walked briskly to the chopper pad only to find it empty. Soon, though, a big Vaught Sikorsky transport helicopter landed on the pad next to us. The rush of wind from the rotors nearly blew our helmets off.

A guy in a blue engineer's cap yelled out the window at us.

"You guys goin' up to Firebase 6?"

"Yeah," I replied.

"Pile in then 'cause that's where I'm heading."

I didn't wait for Lieutenant Martins to join us. I just herded the boys into the Troop Chopper. There was a lot of clunking noise inside as we lifted off. I could feel the old motor of the chopper strain with the weight. I wondered what Firebase 6 was like. We were trimming tops of trees as the Sikorsky Chopper whooshed up country.

Suddenly we heard a sound like hard rain hit the underbelly of the chopper. I head the pilot scream, "Them goddamned Gooks!"

Later I learned it was ground fire that hit the old chopper from below. The pilot said he'd welded a ¾ inch plate of steel on the underside of the chopper.

"They knew they couldn't bring me down, but they shoot at me for their shits and giggles," said the pilot.

I was not amused.

From the air the land was a green canopy interspersed with rice paddies. It didn't look as nasty as it was. Acres and acres of defoliated forest with dead animals lying around. The land groaned heavily under the imprint of war. It was a strange and foreign place with strange and foreign people – all of them strangers to me.

The chopper settled down again on a Landing Zone out in the bush. The pilot's gravelly voice yelled to us, "Get out! Disembark, whatever! This is your destination. Good luck!"

We piled out and stood there watching as he lifted the copter off in a flurry of leaves and dust.

Well. Here we were at Firebase 6.

VIII

Firebase Six

I organized the platoon as best I could, and we laid around for about an hour before we saw three small Vietnamese on bicycles coming toward us. Their pointed woven hats wobbled as they pedaled up the hill. They were dressed in blue and green pajamas and wouldn't look us in the eye as they pulled up.

"Orders!" One shouted and handed me a piece of folded paper. It read: "If you're the new guys, hike on up to the top of the hill. We've moved the base." It was signed Captain Marc Granger. A strange welcome.

One of the men in the platoon yelled at me, "Hey, Egan, is it a birthday party?"

I didn't answer him. I just pointed to the top of the hill and said, "Trek!" We made the climb in loose order. I took no precautions.

"Bang!" shouted a voice from the hilltop. "You're dead!"

I looked up and there was a grizzled looking man about six-foot-tall dressed in a protection flack vest and shorts with flip flops on his feet.

I saluted the two bars on his shoulder. He looked pale and used up.

"Captain Granger?" I asked.

"Yep. This is my dominion," he replied. "Come make yourself at home."

We headed over the hill to a flat area that had scattered yurts and fuel barrels. There was a perimeter of sorts set up and a mess tent. We put up our yurts on the far side of the flat. We weren't exactly made welcome. These guys were Marines, invested in Corps I. Because we were Army, they treated us like we were a burden they had to bear.

"Sir," I said to the Captain. "What are our orders?" I still wasn't clear what a raw platoon of Army Airborne was doing up here.

"Well, Son," he said. "Whenever the Green Berets stir up trouble – you are their team support. In other words, you pull their ass out of the fire."

"And to keep yourselves sharp," he continued. "You get your turn at perimeter patrol starting 0600 tomorrow."

He handed me a pedometer. "Eight clicks out, two clicks over, then eight clicks back. We have two Hmongs to guide you. If you run into Charlie, do not engage."

"Yes, Sir!" I replied, saluted and went to organize my men.

I noticed that we had that bright shiny new look to us - in comparison to the dirty, worn and hollow-eyed look of our fellow Marines. I could see the exhausted Marines resented us from the get-go.

After our camp was in order, I sat by the fire with Willy T.

"I guess that way," he pointed to the Northeast. "Is the great demilitarized zone they talk about?"

"Yeah," I replied. "Seems all smoke and mirrors to me."

As the sun set, I could see the barrenness of Firebase Six, wrapped in barbed concertina wire waiting for an attack. Weary soldiers being held in check by governments thousands of miles away. It was a most depressing thought. I shook my head and dove into my bedroll, collapsing into dreams of a better world.

I was still deep in dreams about Karen and wishing she were here to take the load off my darkened heart when the six o'clock horn blazed. I groaned as I turned out of my bedroll. My senses were hardened as I grabbed my weapon and ammo.

I assembled my platoon and we proceeded to the mess.

The Montagnard (Native North Vietnamese) cooks gave us the unrecognizable flesh of some creature and two cups of rice, not appetizing and not entertaining.

Captain Granger came to the table and sat down with a cup of coffee in his hand. "First out today, I've got two scouts for you to meet. They are Chai and Lai, our Hmong guides. Pick up a pedometer from the quartermaster at supply." He repeated the daily patrol routine, "Eight clicks out, two over, eight clicks back. File a report with me at the end of the day."

Chai and Lai were scouts hired by the U.S. Military to guide troops through their familiar home territory. They were not Military by any stretch of the imagination. They were dressed in shorts, richly colored Hawaiian shirts, rifle, pistol, machete and flip flops.

"Hey, Joe," said this short bush soldier. "Walk in forest?"

"What's your name?" I asked for an opener.

"I'm Chai. That's my brother Lai," he answered. "He don't speak any English, but he's a straight shooter."

"O.K." I said. "I'm Johnny Egan. This is Wilson T, Big Dick, and Left-hand Louie." I introduced the rest of my platoon. I ended with Gary who carried the heavy artillery.

"Uh huh," said Chai in agreement. "Let's go!"

He added a warning, "Little green snake you watch out for, O.K.? They come down out of tree, peck you in the face, you may as well bend over, kiss your ass goodbye."

I wondered what there was to be most afraid of, the V.C. or the crawlies that lived in the bush.

It was a foggy morning. On we went by twos down an old trail, Chai in the lead, Lai bringing up the rear. We'd done about six clicks, according to my little silver pedometer, when Chai halted and held up his hand. He turned around and whispered, "Elephant grass."

I scanned the area and saw we had come to a bare field populated with the nicest little yellow flowers.

"I show you," Chai said. He picked up a rock and threw it out onto the field. The rock sank with an audible slow gurgle.

"Look solid, liquid as hell," Chai pronounced. "Go on that, be a week before they find your body. We go around."

We tromped around the field looking out for tree snakes. In another couple of clicks I reset the pedometer and on we went, still walking through the fog. At two o'clock we rested.

"Ow! I'm hit!" Yelled one of the Corps men. It was Branscom.

"Return fire!" I yelled. All I could see were muzzle flashes and fog. I got behind a log and fired into the mist. There were screams returned from the shadowy forest. I heard Gary's artillery B.A.R. (Browning Automatic Rifle) join in with a whoosh, then all went quiet. So much for the non-engagement I had been told by the Captain.

"Jeezus Christ, Boss!" said Chai. He had hunkered down behind the comfortable log with me. "What the hell was that?" he asked.

"Someone who didn't like us," I said.

A voice in the distance started yelling, "*No doc toi! No doc toi!*"

"What's he saying," I asked Chai.

"Means he won't shoot," answered Chai. "I think he wants a parley."

"Come ahead," I yelled back at the unknown man.

A small figure in black pajamas walked into the clearing, his rifle held above his head. He threw it on the ground, smiled at us, then pulled a dead man switch and blew himself into little black and red bits.

The concussion of his blast knocked me off my feet. None of my men were hurt, but my ears rang for hours.

"Good Lord," I exclaimed, shaking my head. "What the hell is wrong with these guys! They could have laid low and let us go by and we'd never been the wiser."

Chai responded, "They spirited by the ghost of Ho Chi Minh. You are White devils to them."

"We'd better get a chopper out here to take the Corps man to Med," I ordered. "Anybody else hurt or wounded?" Then I heard a series of grunts, groans and 'Nos' from different corners.

"Let's check their boys." I said. "Get a head count."

Lai went tripping into the forest. He came back within ten minutes and said something to Chai.

We got twenty-four of them," Chai told me. "Better get their guns and ammo. Everybody knows their AK's better than M16s. You can fire them with mud in the barrel and they still shoot. M16 piece of shit. Jam in the middle of firefight! Leave you high and dry."

Chai was right. You had to keep a condom over the barrel of an M16 to keep it dry in wet country, and you had to clean your weapon in the field every day if you didn't want it to jam on you. M16s were Americans' piece of shit.

The chopping sounds of the helicopter rotors came in hard and heavy. They landed in the clearing next to the battle site and whisked Private Branscom away. I had Left Hand-Louie go with him to make sure they didn't treat him like a piece of meat.

We trekked back to Fire Base Six; it had been a good day on patrol.

"I thought I said not to engage!" Captain Granger shouted at me in anger. "Now you've offed twenty-four of the buggars! Not a good start, Egan!"

I looked him straight in the eye and said, "Sir, they attacked us. Are we not supposed to defend ourselves?"

Then he grunted. "I suppose," he said. "Sorry. This job is getting to me. You did a good job with only one casualty on our side. Carry on!"

There was growing unrest in Fire Base Six. The Captain was in touch with Fire Base 4 and 5 and they too were experiencing small bands of V.C. sneaking through the jungle. The V.C. were trying to establish a supply road to the South from the North. The land groaned again under the stress of war.

Every day my boys and I were sent out to beat the bushes for Charlie.

One day in November of 1968 we were walking through tall stalks of what looked like cut grass. I forget what they called that stuff. Condoms were on the barrels of our guns to prevent crap getting in the barrels. Suddenly there was the chatter of gun fire and we hit the ground. No one cried out in pain and then someone shouted from our ranks which told me my platoon was intact.

"What the hell is going on?" cried Willie T.

"I dunno but I don't think they're shooting at us."

"By twos," I yelled at my men. That meant that each man moved in a phalanx toward the trouble, one man back up the other. At the edge of the jungle we suddenly saw a platoon of our guys in retreat. Captain Granger was in command.

About fifty V.C. had ambushed them and only the Captain was holding those brave Marines from cutting and running.

I could see the V.C. didn't know we were in their locale, so I motioned to Left-Hand Louis and Big Dick to circle toward the right with four boys each. When the V.C. broke cover we let them have it. we had them in a crossfire, and they went down like mowed grass.

Then it happened! I was wading through the tall grass to link up with Captain Granger and this little S.O.B. popped up in front of me with a Bolo machete in his hand. He took a wild swipe at me and cut a rip through my flak vest. My odd thought was, "How rude!" and then shot him.

At close range I could see the hopelessness in his eyes as life left his body. I wanted to puke.

I walked up to Captain Granger and saluted.

He had a shocked look on his face as he said, "Soldier, you're bleeding."

I looked down and the whole of my right side was soaked in blood. My own. That little fucker had chopped me neat as a surgeon under my right arm.

"Piss!" I said and passed out.

The next thing I remember was coming to in the back of a chopper and a Corps man making me hold a pressure bandage under my right arm. I was lying down.

"You got nicked, Soldier," the Corps man said. "You're going to Nha Trang and they'll fix you up."

My arm was stiff, and my wound hurt. I was dirty and I didn't feel like pleasant company, but I sat up and wriggled into one of the seats. I didn't want to be lying down. I felt like half a man with my arm all wrapped up over my chest.

We landed on the Med-transfer pad and three husky nurses escorted me to the surgery tent. After I had been lying there for some time, a doctor came in; George Amos, his I.D. said.

"Let's take a look at this," were his only words to me. He was clean cut, about twenty-five years old. I remember he had very clean fingernails.

"We're going to have to take that sweat gland out," he finally said. "It's going to hurt."

"Explain," I demanded.

"Well," he said. "This looks like one deep slice wound. They are often poisoned. It hasn't spread up to now, but the gland is compromised. If we deaden you up, that could cause that crap to push through your system and kill you. We have to pluck that bugger out before it has a chance to."

The nurse stuck a tongue depressor wrapped with tape into my mouth. I bit down as the doctor made his move. I heard a rip and I screamed with pain - the worst I'd ever experienced. I shut my eyes and was lightheaded for some time.

The doctor held up the remnants of my sweat gland in his hand and looked at me, breathing a sigh of relief.

"Now we cannot close up that wound," the doc said. "It will have to close up naturally."

Twenty-four hours later a chopper transported me back to Fire Base Six.

For the next three weeks I went around with an open wound under my arm which I slathered daily with neomycin and I was required to stuff wadding into the hole and then bandage it.

The captain smiled at me and said, "Well, I guess you got your first purple heart Egan. Orders say you've got light duty."

I went to my yurt and Willy T. was there.

"God, I thought we'd lost you," he said.

"I was hoping for a ticket home," I replied in jest.

"You're not so fucking lucky," Left-hand Louie said as he entered. "Here's your rifle. I been cleaning it for you."

"Thank you Soldier," I said. He turned on his heels and walked away.

IX

Dinner with Chai

Then on to Ahn Lok

The days became tedious. It was dead at Fire Base Six. Patrols were slowed to every other day. Those mighty Marines started taking their turn at patrolling, so we did not have as much work to do.

This was our day to do the rounds. It was a hot and muggy day, a typical South Vietnam day. Yes, very hot, then stifling muggy. The platoon was on the way back from Con Lai on its daily patrol. We were being led by Chai and Lai. Left-hand Louie was near the center of our line when he decided to take a short cut by himself off the trail through some jungle undergrowth - Banana leaves and ground cover of many twisted vines.

Chai turned to look at Louie and his eyes got really big. He approached Louie with his twelve-and-a-half-foot bladed knife raised over his head. As Louie went past, Chai stabbed straight down atop

Louie's helmet and picked off a huge tarantula the size of a dinner plate, still wriggling on the end of the knife in its death throes. All of this was unbeknownst to Louie who remained oblivious to the whole thing.

Chai said loudly, "Good dinner! Good dinner!" And plopped it in his side bag.

When we got back to Firebase 6, Chai enthusiastically dug a hole about 3 foot around and 2 ½ foot deep. He put two big rocks into our day fire (which was always burning). After heating the rocks for about an hour they appeared to be red hot. Chai shoveled the rocks into the hole with about ten gallons of water. It was boiling instantly. Then he took the tarantula out of his bag and threw it in the water. In fifteen minutes, the tarantula turned pink, just like a cooked crab. With his long knife Chai extracted the tarantula from the water. Then he went to the fire and singed off all the wiry pieces of hair all over the surface of the spider.

"Don't want to eat the hair," Chai said to me, "Because it will kill you deader than hell!"

He broke off a couple of the legs as he said, "Hey you, Johnny. Here, just eat the inside…it tastes just like crab! Mmm."

My thought was -A new Vietnamese delicacy…I'll try it once. No one else opted to try it. I don't think I'll ever eat that again.

I recalled in the big cities in the open-air markets they also had fried scorpions. Cooked in a wok, covered with soy sauce. They were very like shrimp, deep fried then placed on skewers. Stingers were left on till the person eating them removed the shell casing and the stinger. The poison, still in the stinger, was thrown away.

They also ate grasshoppers – locusts a foot-long, deep fried, cooked in a huge wok. A pile placed in a paper bag were then eaten like French fries. On one outing Willie T. dared me, "I bet you won't eat that!" I took his dare and ate one, that was enough for me.

Dinner time was over. Orders came through from Command that a special secret operation was to take place and McCord's Raiders were to be part of it.

We were moved by chopper back to Nha Trang. I was growing to hate that place. Colonel Ashton filled me in on our assignment. It seemed the Cambodians were running a slave camp with a bunch of our pilots that had been captured after they had been shot down. Six Green Beret men and our platoon were supposed to get the pilots out. The dicey thing about it was that it was in Cambodia, and we weren't at war with them – yet.

I knew when Nixon was elected in the U.S.A. that things in Viet Nam would go from bad to worse. We'd seen pictures of the riots on Captain Granger's T.V. He could get a T.V. signal from Saigon. We saw Jack Kennedy killed, then Dr. King. The world seemed to be turning into shit and we were stuck right in the asshole of the world. What did we do about it? We followed orders.

Six Green Berets and our fourteen LRP (Long Range Patrol) Support guys were about to invade Cambodia in secret.

It was 1200 hours, about midnight. Twenty of us loaded into a chopper bound for a little village called Ahn Lok. The radio chatter was about the rescue helicopters we were waiting for. We needed to be sure not to get stuck in Cambodian airspace because that would create an international incident.

Other Green Berets had already been through the area. We were dumped on the top of a ridge overlooking a quaint bunch of huts and rice paddies. I signaled silently to my men to go by twos, and thus we crept into town.

There was no one to be seen. The village had been deserted for some time. I was totally puzzled until the whole Cambodian Army came over the hill ready to harvest our scalps.

I screamed as loud as I could, "It's a set up! Get the chopper back here and get us outta here!" then I saw Randy, our radio man. He just shook his head and yelled back, "They can't come into Cambodian airspace!"

I could hear the sputtered chatter of A.K.s starting at us from beyond the village limits. I had to make a decision immediately.

"Head for the river," I yelled at the men. "Randy, see if you can get us some help!"

We tried an orderly retreat, again by twos supporting one another like our training had taught us but soon it became impossible, and every man was running to save his own ass. If we were captured, we might spend ten years in some Cambodian slave farm having to do God knows what to survive.

Randy shouted at me again. "I got the Navy!"

"What did they say?" I shouted back.

"They said get to the river and they'll send us a Swiftboat.

I had seen Swiftboats. They were floating armories. That could be our salvation.

We hustled down a small trail that led to the edge of the Mekong. There were tall grasses, cat tails and tangled jungle trees, all sorts of stuff to climb through. We finally found ourselves wading in the water.

All of a sudden there was a roar and rush of water and into sight came a Swiftboat.

A sailor shouted at us, "Duck! Get down!" They pulled into position as we ducked. Then they let loose with four banks of sixty-millimeter chain guns - the kind that puts a bullet every half inch apart and can clear a trail in the jungle for you.

"WHA HOO!" The sailor shouted. "Look at those piggy-eyed squints run!"

"Grab a rope Army. Let's get you outta here!"

We swam out to meet them and they threw a rope to each of us. The downside of this was that the boat started out of the site before they pulled us aboard. They dragged us a quarter of a mile downstream before they could reel us in. We were a bedraggled bunch as we got back into Vietnamese waters.

One of the sailors on the Swiftboat asked me "What'd you guys be doin' up in Cambodia?"

"Can't say," I said. "Top secret."

Top secret my ass. I was so pissed at the brass that I could have stood them up against a wall and shot them. What a snafu situation. Normal for them, all screwed up!

December 1968, and as usual it was raining. A monsoon had pushed in over Nha Trang and beat the hell out of the land. Thunder, lightning, and wind at 100 miles an hour. We hunkered down in an old barracks on the east side of Nha Trang. I'd never seen such a storm. It seemed the gods were angry all at once for what was going on over here. Big Dick came running across the parade grounds to me.

"Johnny," he shouted. "They got a couple of whores across the way. They're screwing the whole platoon for $20 American apiece. Come and get some!"

His enthusiasm made me cringe. "No," I said firmly. I was thinking about how many of those men would get a dose of clap or something worse from one of those loose Saigon whores. I told him, "I've still got my right hand."

"You don't know what you're missing," Big Dick said. "You ain't got laid since Manila."

"And I ain't got no dose of their diseases either." Then I pointed in the direction of the Medical facility just east of us. He left me in my moodiness.

X

I felt dreary. I was so down by then that the prospect of getting shot and sent home was not all that unattractive. True, they had given me my first purple heart and another stripe on my shoulder – but I knew bullshit when I got mixed up in it and this was the worst bullshit.

The typhoon blew over and it was blistering hot in December. We were again stationed at Fire Base Six.

Good morning!" Captain Granger said brightly. He looked at our platoon and said, "It's good to see your smiling faces in hell again."

"Yes Sir!" I blurted out with a sneer.

"I see that you are carrying another stripe on your shoulder, Egan," he replied. "Will that shut you up now that you're an E6?"

"Not hardly," I said. "My enlistment is up in March."

"Well then," he answered my attitude with his. "Let's hope you survive it." He went off to his tent where his private whore and a snuff of opium awaited him. He said that the two of them helped him get through the day.

I heard Gary, our B.A.R. man muttering to himself. I noticed it was right after one of those light planes called a Caribou flew over us.

"What's the matter, Gary?" I asked him.

"Goddam CIA bastards," he replied. "They fly into the interior and buy their peace with heroin. Not even the N.V.A. will mess with the drug lord's over there."

"I'm no fan of the CIA," I said. "But what's wrong with a little peace?"

"It's not that," Gary responded. "They bring junk back to our boys and make them stone cold addicts. My brother got hooked. He got hooked so bad that he took a .45 and made a canoe out of his own head. It's really bad shit, and those guys are bad people.

He went back to cleaning his gun. I could see his point.

It was three days later, and we were prepared for another romp in the jungle. Chai and Lai were our guides again and Chai said he had a special treat for us. He spoke with delight.

"We make snake today for dinner!" He had whacked the head off of a big King Brown snake, had already skinned it and cut it into steaks.

Our mission was to head down the river and hangout looking for jungle traffic heading south. The brass was afraid too many heavy weapons were being smuggled through the small village of Lin Bo that sat just shy of the river.

One of our favorite nicknames was "Louie" for Lieutenant. This time though we had or own Louie with us who had just joined our two platoons. Lieutenant Lindly Becker. He was our leader and a pompous fool.

We tromped out at daylight on the way to Lin Bo. The whole place had been leveled four or five times, but the residents kept returning and rebuilding the rag tag village. It was our job to find out why.

The first night in the jungle Chai built a small fire and toasted his snake on small spits for us. It was actually delicious and tasted much like chicken.

Lindly Becker complained a lot about the cooking fire giving our position away to the enemy.

Chai laughed at him. "They know where we are the minute we hit the jungle. That's no mystery. It's all in whether they want to fight or not. Don't be silly. The snake is good this way."

As night came on we all picked two trees that grew close together and set up our hammocks. It was safer in the trees so snakes and crawly things wouldn't disturb our sleep. The jungle floor is full of life at night and it all bites or stings. Our guard was set up and it started to rain.

The next day dawned. The sun in the east made the jungle look like some post card from paradise. We were then about five miles from Lin Bo. We started to get sniper fire from the left. No one was injured so I figured the enemy was just trying to draw our attention. We kept on slogging toward Lin Bo.

About half a mile from the gates of Lin Bo, (we were then calling them 'gates'), there was a road that led through the high, thick hedge that surrounded the village.

We started taking on more fire. We returned fire and heard the enemy retreat past the village. They were trying to draw us away into the jungle. All around us went deadly still.

"They've run away," Lieutenant Lindley Becker said. "Now's our chance to capture the village!"

"Sir," I said. "There is a better way than that road. If we go down the road they can pick us off like targets as we come out."

"Nonsense," Lindley Becker said firmly. He threw his chest out, straightened his back, grabbed his rifle and started down the road toward the gate. He was about six steps down the road when his head disappeared, helmet and all. His body fell into a mass of his own blood! The platoon men had stopped at my words. We all looked on with the ever-present fear. I shook my head. So arrogant Lindley Becker was killed by his own stupidity.

I was then in command. I separated our two platoons and came at the village from the sides. It was an old Zulu trick I'd learned called the 'horns of the bull.'

We cleared out the Charlie (enemy) that were in the village. We didn't capture many of them, five I think. We disarmed them and tied them up, placed them in a circle. I ordered our men to scour the village and see what was so damned important about this place to Charlie.

Willie T. discovered it. "The damned ground rings hollow over here!" He shouted. Upon further investigation we discovered the whole place was honey-combed with tunnels. It was a huge weapons cache. All around the village we found tunnels. One we uncovered had about a ton of plastic explosives in it.

"That'll do it," I thought out loud.

"Anybody got a satchel charge?" I yelled out.

Art Peabody yelled back, "I've got three!"

"We'll link them up to the C4," I said. "And that ought to send this whole place up."

Art was very good at rigging explosives. He told me his dad was an underwater demolitions expert and he had learned from him.

Three of Lieutenant Lindley Becker's men dragged his body back to a place where a chopper could pick it up, and then the rest of us backed away from Lin Bo.

When Art touched off the satchel charges the C4 went too. It rained little pieces of the village for an hour and when it all settled, what was left was a hole in the ground twenty feet deep and a hundred yards wide in the Vietnam landscape.

I thought what a stupid waste it was for Lieutenant Lindley Becker to have died there. When it came down to it he died from his ignorance and arrogance. He would have made the perfect military lifer and retired with a small blonde woman with three kids of his own making back in the states, but he opted to be a hero.

As we marched back to Fire Base Six we encountered a lot of the Vietnamese people who lived in the area who had before remained invisible. They dropped their eyes to the ground when we looked at them, except for a very few.

What really got to me was the way they brought children into the world.

We were about two miles from this village Con Lai when we heard the screaming of a woman in labor. Two other women helped her lean against a tree, and she squatted down. The child, the afterbirth and everything came tumbling out of her like a hard bowel movement. As I stood at a distance watching, I was amazed. Three hours later I knew she was back to work in the rice paddy, up to her knees in the muddy water, her baby swinging from a cloth wrap and stuck to her breast, sucking contentedly. What a way to live!

XI

A Hard Day

Six miles on the other side of Con Lai we ran into serious resistance. They were North Vietnamese Regulars; tanks and all. They were headed south to establish an inroad for other Regulars coming behind them.

Then there were our groups. Marines and ARVN (Army of Viet Nam). I reported to a Captain whose name I cannot remember. He told me to turn in Lindley Becker's bars of rank with his dog tags to the man in the supply tent.

"Jesus, it's been hot here!" The captain said. "They've been shooting it out for three days. They're determined little bastards.

He went on to say, "I Core sent for help from our tanks and they arrived yesterday, but it's unclear who has the upper hand."

"Wonderful," I said. "I got my Lieutenant's bars and tags for you."

"There's a typewriter in back," he said as he took the tags. "Type me up a brief version of events." He handed me two pieces of typewriter paper. I went to the back of the supply tent, fished out an old Underwood manual with a bad ribbon. I put it on two ammo boxes and typed.

I was ordered to take and destroy the village of Lin Bo. In the action Lieutenant Linley Becker was hit and killed by enemy fire. We took and destroyed Lin Bo completely. Mission accomplished.

As I handed my report to the sergeant I said, "I was brief."

"Good," he replied. "I've got a stack for HQ and this just goes in the pile."

"Do you know where Captain Granger is?" I queried.

"Yeah, North West section 4," he said. He pointed in a vague direction north of where we stood.

I rounded up my guys, Willie T., Big Dick, Gary, Left-Hand Louie and what was left of our platoon. We had now lost two men. We trekked northwest to meet up with Granger. This sector was alive with traffic. Choppers were buzzing overhead, and we could hear the pop-pop of AK's going off in the distance. We needed a radio. Left-Hand Louie found one and we were soon in contact with Captain Granger.

"Get your ass up here, Egan!" He squawked. "We need every gun you've got!"

"On our way!" I shouted into the microphone and off we went.

Granger was some sixteen miles away, fighting with Vietnamese Regulars that had crossed the DMZ. The only way we could get there was to flag down a Huey Helicopter and hitch a ride. Huey's were everywhere; they were open-doored battle copters converted for whatever need and purpose of the moment.

I saw a guy I knew, Rafe Goodman, filling his Huey with the jet fuel they used for those things.

"Hey Rafe!" I yelled and he turned around with a quizzical look.

"I know you don't I?" he said. "Egan, ain't it?"

"Yeah, that's me. It's been awhile," I said.

"Whew!" he exclaimed. "They got you down here beatin' the brush too. I thought you'd be shining a stool up in D.C. or something."

"Not hardly," I replied. "But one can hope."

"Watcha need, buddy?" he asked.

"Can you get me and my platoon, or what's left of it, up to Sector 4?"

"Sure. Me and my guys have to chase NVA in Sector 6. You can hitch a ride; it's live action up that way though. Don't know why you'd wanna get there."

"The usual thing," I said. "Orders."

We loaded into the hull of his copter and elbowed the gunner aside. His name was Skinner, a quiet type who frowned at us to let us know he didn't like our group hitch hiking.

We lifted off and in about twenty minutes we were in Sector 4.

"I've got a good LZ 'bout a quarter of a mile from Granger," Rafe yelled over the loud engines. "You're on your own from there."

"Thanks!" I yelled back at him. "Better late than never!"

We tumbled out at our destination and Rafe took off in his Huey in a flurry of dust and churned up leaves. He grinned and waved at me. I never saw him again. I hope he survived, did his time and went back to the States and settled down.

There was a long low field of elephant grass between us and Granger. It was the dry season, as dry as it ever gets there, so I figured we could scout the edge of the grass and come up on his left flank.

"Is that you Egan?" I heard Granger on the radio.

I responded, "We got a lift, Sir. Sorry we're late, Sir."

"Well get your ass over here," he said. "Somebody gave the Gooks tracer rounds. They've taken out half my guys!"

Just about then I saw a stream of tracers arc toward us. I felt a sting at the back of my elbow. Apparently, one had just clipped my arm.

Aloud I said, "Ow!"

It burned but there was no blood. It had cauterized the wound right then and there. My arm swelled up and turned purple by the wound. Half an hour later it hurt like a son-of-a-bitch.

We came in on the enemy's left flank. Just our few guns made them scatter and run.

As we reached Granger the Marines were mopping up and there were several choppers transferring prisoners.

Captain Granger came up to me. "That's the second time you've pulled my ass out of the toilet Egan. It's getting to be a habit." He smiled and then looked concerned. "Soldier, you're bleeding again."

"I took one under the elbow out in the field as we were approaching, Sir," I told him.

He yelled out, "Medic!" and a very young Corps man came up from somewhere and had me roll up my sleeve.

"Jesus!" he exclaimed. "Never seen a wound like this before! It's cauterized."

He slapped a handful of neomycin on it, then a pressure bandage.

"You're getting to be Charlie's favorite target," Captain Granger said.

"Things will be quiet for the next week or two," Granger continued. "The ARVN isn't ready for a real push."

As he was walking away Granger asked, "Egan, have you ever had a furlough?"

"No, Captain. I haven't," I replied.

"Well, I'm sending you on one," he said. "Two weeks. Go to Bangkok. Get laid. Tie a good one on. See my secretary back at Sector 6." He smiled crookedly at me. "It ain't all about this god-damned war. Take a buddy with you."

I talked with my four closest buddies, Willie T., Big Dick, Gary and Left-Hand Louie.

"The Captain's sending me on a hoot," I told them. "He said to kick up my heels and I gotta take one of you with me. We're going to draw straws."

"How about matches?" suggested Willie T. "I got a pack from a fruit merchant down the road."

"Okay, give them to me," I said as I snatched them out of his hand. "Person who gets the short match gets to go."

I put one short match among several long ones in my hand.

"Hey! It's Louie!" shouted Willie T after Louie came up with the short match. "And we get to be Marines for a couple of weeks." Everyone frowned him down at that prospect.

It took a good deal of wiggling to get furlough orders from the secretary at Fire Base 6, but after the secretary had a few radio conversations with Captain Granger yelling, "Fix the fucking orders!" the secretary handed Louie and me two pieces of paper mostly saying if we weren't back by 1/29/69 we were AWOL.

We hitched a chopper ride to Nha Trang and rode Troop Transport to Saigon.

Saigon was a big city, not quite a big as L.A. but from the air you couldn't see where it ended, and countryside began. There were people, so many they seemed to me to be squashed back to front everywhere, no space between them. Louie and I played tourist and hit the bars while waiting for a plane to take us to Bangkok, Thailand.

XII

Bangkok

Even before we got out of Viet Nam, "What you want, Joe?" was the most frequent comment thrown at us in broken English.

One thing we especially noticed were the beautiful "sweeping women" who were ferried around in Limousines.

"Who are they?" I asked one bartender.

"Convent girls," he replied. "Part Viet and part French. The nuns rescue them when they are babies. They don't let them out without a guard."

"Why is that?" I asked naively.

"Somebody will pop 'em off if they ain't guarded," he continued. He saw the question in my eyes and said, "Because they're only half Viet. It is against our culture to have half white babies."

I learned that racial prejudice was firm in that country and what I had seen thus far in my life, it looked to me to be worldwide.

Louie and I boarded the plane that took us into Thailand, Bangkok International Airport. The nicely dressed stewardess were urban, polite and all very pretty.

Louie fell in love with one of them instantly. Her name tag said she was Mai Lin.

It took about an hour to fly from Saigon to Bangkok. Now that was a city! You could see from the air that it was a huge city in the shape of a circle. It had a big muddy river running through it, and like Saigon, you could not see the countryside around it because it was so wide.

To us it seemed peaceful except for the few arrogant military police who were present. They gave the idea of enforcement of law and order.

As we deboarded the plane we found crowds of foreigners like ourselves wandering around and gaping at everything.

The oddest thing was the flesh merchants ever present calling out their wares.

"Hey Joe! Only 3500 bat for virgin from the farm country."

Louie gave a disgusted look and I laughed.

"It's the Far East, Louie. You can buy anything here!"

We were searched as we got off the plane. The inspectors were polite in this case.

"Any weapons, Joe?"

We shrugged a 'No' and the inspector said, "Have a good time; enjoy Thailand."

We had changed our American money into bat, the Thai currency, before we left Saigon. I felt rich with $20 American made into 60,000 bat. And women! They were all beautiful and all available for a price. I thought Louie was going to trip over his boot laces taking them all in.

"I wonder," muttered Louie, "If Mai Li from the airplane was up for sale or rent?"

I laughed again. "Probably, but only for U.S. dollars, my friend,"

We strolled around the airport and found a Hilton Hotel Kiosk. The little Thai man spoke to us with a perfect British accent and booked us a room right then. We hailed a pedicab, you know, the guy on a bicycle pulling a carrier wagon on the back.

We settled back then but it was only a twist, a turn and we were now in front of the Bangkok Hilton and booked into room 211.

A good-looking young Thai boy about sixteen years old grabbed our bags and then we were in the room overlooking the river. I tipped him 40 bat and his eyes went wide.

"Anything you want, Joe," the boy recited. "Women, drugs, booze. You call for me, I get." He held out a name tag that had 'Adrew' printed on it.

I smiled at him and the quaint spelling of his name as he left us.

Louie was already lying on his bed watching T.V. We didn't get much of that back on Fire Base 6.

He smiled at me from his bed. "I'm good, Sarge," he said. He was looking at the news. "You know they elected Nixon President back in the U.S.?"

"Yeah Louie," I said flatly. "I knew." Then I told him, "I'm headed down to the restaurant to see if I can get a steak. Don't go out without leaving me a note as to where you intend to be going."

"Yes, boss," he replied absent mindedly. As I went out the door, I wished I had added, "That's an order."

The elevator took me down to the restaurant. It was clean and new and the food was sumptuous. It almost seemed like the war and all its ruin were a bad dream I had left behind. I took the tourist tour without Louie. It was mostly scantily clad Britishers at my elbow, saying ohh and ahh as they pointed at the ancient religious statues. I got off the tour bus at a place that was marked as 'Change Alley.' The little tour guide kept shaking his head no and trying to persuade me to get back on the bus and stay with the tour.

In his pidgin English he kept repeating, "No go in there!" but I waved him off.

Change Alley ran along the banks of the Irrawaddy River. Thousands of people crowded along the banks living on spring-lined boats docked at the shore. The population was all Thai people. I found the reason the tour guide tried to coax me not to go there - if you had anything of value on your body it would be gone by the time you had passed through to the end of the alley. Many people had the strange sly look of poverty who were willing to do anything for a few bat.

I heard a gun go off. BANG! I looked up to see one of those arrogant little Thai Military Police standing over the corpse of a fisherman. He looked at me and said in perfect English, "He was a thief and a murderer. He was about to murder you for whatever you have in your pockets."

I didn't ask any questions. I let the MP escort me back to the main tourist drag, away from Change Alley.

"Have a good visit to Bangkok," he smiled.

I decided to stick to the main tourist spots after that.

I spotted a motor peddy cab, this one a small motorcycle with a cab attached that let the driver roll me around Bangkok for forty bat. A lot to see, especially the Buddhist temples. The king's palace also struck me as beautiful.

I got back to room 211 at the Bangkok Hilton, opened the door to find Louie was not alone. The beautiful Mai Li was sitting beside him on the sofa with only a towel wrapped around her.

"How?" I started to ask, but Mai Li interrupted.

"Louie is a very generous guy and cute too."

Louie was grinning from ear to ear. He said, "I guess some wishes come true, huh Sarge."

I went through to my adjacent room and flopped down on the bed, exhausted.

Mai Li proved to be the best tour guide we could have. She took us up-country and all around the city in a rented car.

Louie and Mai Li seemed to be madly in love, and Louie told me he intended to take her back to the States as his wife. I was glad for him.

We spent ten days on the bum, doing nothing. Louie and Mai Li were in the bedroom most of the time and when it came time for us to go back to Viet Nam, she cried.

"I don't expect she'll stay true to me," Louie said, "but when this war is done for me, she's willing to come back to the States with me."

I said playfully, "If we survive," but it was an apparent truth.

We de-planed in Saigon and were amazed at all the troops around us, both our U.S. troops and the ARVN. If was full-blown war again for us and gearing back up to being shot at was difficult.

"Let's get a beer," said Louie. "There's a place over by that shoeshine boy. He pointed to a little cubby hole bar across the street from the big glass doors of the Saigon Airport Terminal.

"Sounds good," I replied. "Our transport won't be here for another hour to take us back to our unit."

Louie was excited. He had a month and twenty day left on his enlistment and was due to go back to the States after that.

"I'm going to get Mai Li and split this hole," he said. "My dad's got a farm in Orange County. We'll settle down and raise fat Thai children." His smile was still on his face.

The bar, small as it was, was packed with older Vietnamese who were dressed in uniforms of the Airport workmen. We were given a seat in the back of the dimly lit bar. We sipped our beer and were quiet with our own thoughts.

"I'm going to get a shine on these old boots," Louie said. "I ain't had one of those forever." He rose from his chair as he said, "There's that kid out front." He went out the door. I sat still wondering what this war was all about.

Suddenly there was a huge "KA BOOM!"

The windows of the bar caved inward, glass flying everywhere. Several of the old workmen were badly cut.

I rushed out the front door looking for Louie.

There he was laying up against the outside wall of the bar, dead as dead. The blast had taken his leg off at the hip and killed him instantly. I walked over and bent down to shut his eyes. The blast had blown the shoeshine boy all the way across the street. He was dead too, plastered up against a shattered window. The ARVN was there in seconds and had me at gunpoint jabbering at me in Vietnamese. Within fifteen minutes the Army Contingent arrived.

A snooty lieutenant asked me what happened. I was angry. "Don't be a damned fool, Lieutenant," I said. "Louie went out to get a damned shoeshine and the box was wired and it blew him to hell."

"Be civil, Sergeant!" he barked back at me. "Or I'll throw you in the brig for gross negligence!"

Simultaneously I saw my Troop Transport pull up.

I calmed myself a bit and replied, "Don't be an asshole if you can help it, Sir."

He moved to grab me, but my transport guys pulled me away from him. I doubled over by the truck and vomited. You'd think I'd be used to it by now, death and mayhem, but it all just made me sick. So much blood! It puddled in the street turning black with oxygenation. The last thing I remembered was an old woman nearby holding one of her hands in pain.

The dull hum of the Transport was hypnotic. I kept reliving the part where I shut Louie's eyes. The road bumped along beneath me and eventually I fell asleep.

"We are at Nha Trang," a voice yelled to me. I roused myself, took a deep breath and got out. I went in search of my commanding officer. His name was Captain Clifford Hilleman. He didn't command much that I could see but pushed numbers around while shining his padded chair with his ass.

I made my report to his little WAC secretary who typed it up. From Hilleman I got a nod and a "See you later." He was a lifer who was said to have been at Omaha Beach at Normandy. He whisked me in and out of his office in twenty minutes and you could see he didn't give a good god-damn about one casualty.

I walked across the old landing strip where they parked the tanks and went to housing. I saw the 82nd Airborne's Lightning and Eagle Insignia and went in. The sergeant assigned me a bunk, gave me a coupon to take to Supply and get outfitted again.

I sat down in the nearby café and wrote to Mai Li about Louie's incident. I posted it to the address in Bangkok that she had given me. Then I hopped in a chopper going back to Fire Base 6. I kept thinking what a lousy stinking place this was.

XIII

More Grief

As I walked up to Fire Base 6 my legs felt like lead. I was moving very slowly. I did not want to tell the guys of my platoon about losing Louie. Captain Granger caught me just before I went into the mess tent.

"Tough break back there, Egan," Granger said. "Regimental already briefed us. You don't have to say a word."

I stood straight and saluted him. He was a hell of a man.

The eyes of my men were enough. They all gathered around me, their eyes grown hard with this war. One by one they said they were sorry. Chai, our Montagnard scout, put his hand on my shoulder, looked deep into my eyes and said, "Someday there will be peace and these things will be only memories."

I went into my yurt and fell in bed. Technically I had twelve more hours of leave and I hoped to sleep for the rest of it.

Morning came and I assembled my platoon for another day of scouting run around of Fire Base 6. This time our eight clicks were to the south, southeast of the base. Our luck seemed to have drained away that day. We ran into elephants – real elephants. They were a smaller kind than we had seen, but more vicious. They chased Chai up a tree and rumbled through our section of the jungle doing a great deal of damage. We thought a tank had been through the place.

"Why don't you just shoot 'em?" Willie T. asked.

"No, no!" whined Chai. "They are sacred. It would be like shooting own mother!"

He continued, "We go 'round them."

It was difficult to get around them, but we managed.

Chai was proud of himself that day. He had stolen a Laws Rocket from the base and carried it like a prideful possession. The Laws Rocket was a one-shot disposable rocket powerful enough to take out a tank.

"Everything is plastic nowadays," I speculated. But to Chai I said, "Be careful of that thing."

"Yes, Boss," Chai responded with a wink.

I knew trouble would come of it and it did. We were about a half mile from a little village called Pli Lo. The people were friendly to whomever had the most fire power at the time.

The village people came out when they saw us and tried to give us rice. In the past they had shown a preference when we traded MRE's with them, the 'meals-ready-to-eat' that we carried. These meals were not our favorite. To describe an MRE, it was a foil package that one had to pull off a strip that set up a chemical reaction to heat the contents. For us they were better than nothing, but not by much. MRE's came in two flavors, beef or chicken.

Anyway, we got rid of a lot of them at Pli Lo, which was also the route the CIA Caribou planes chose to pass over into the interior. The CIA guys traded heroin with Vietnamese for favors so the enemy's boys didn't come down on our boys.

The sad part about it was it made heroin dirt cheap and a lot of our men got hooked on it. Gary Pasquini's brother had been hooked and Gary hated the CIA with a passion because of the drug trading issue.

One day as we were doing our scouting, Gary had to go into the bush to relieve himself. Our platoon didn't think much about it, but after ten minutes or so waiting for his return we began to wonder where he was.

The forest was quiet, just a few bird calls and the slow drone of one of the Caribou Planes. All of a sudden, we heard a huge WHOOSH! BANG!

We looked up and saw the caribou plane come apart almost over our heads. It descended into the jungle in a ball of flame. Just then Gary came back into our group with a shit-eating grin on his face.

Chai started chattering about his Laws Rocket. He was hunting everywhere. We saw that he couldn't find the Rocket anywhere.

"But I laid it down right here," he insisted and pointed to a rotten log he'd been sitting on.

"Things walk around here," I said. "If you don't tie them down."

Everyone stood around and held up their hands; no Laws Rocket to be seen. Chai was grumpy for a while.

We went out into the jungle area and checked out the wreck. Marty, our new radio man phoned it in. Command told us we were to leave and get to Fire Base 6. Of the Caribou plane crew - there were no survivors.

As we plodded up the hill at Fire Base 6, we noticed a Huey on the copter pad. It had CIA painted on the side. Every one of us was herded into the mess tent only to see two guys with white pin stripped shirts and sunglasses waiting for us.

They didn't introduce themselves. They just started firing questions at us.

"What did you see?"

"When did you see it?"

"Who was out there?"

I was proud of my platoon; nobody saw anything but the plane go down.

"You realize that you can all go to the brig for twenty years if you are withholding evidence?" The CIA investigators said sternly. Still no one saw anything.

Finally I said, "I speak for my platoon, and myself. All I saw was the plane catch fire in the sky and explode as it fell to the ground. You can take that back to Langley or wherever." I turned to go and one of the CIA men said, "You are not dismissed."

"I am tired, and I don't see any bars on your shoulder that tell me I should take orders from you. Talk to my Captain."

My whole platoon emptied out of the mess tent and to our respective yurts. I chuckled inside myself. I knew that Gary had finally exacted his revenge for his brother's addiction on the CIA.

XIII

Border Crossings

It was early in March of 1969, and things were cruising along as usual. We were getting shot at and obeying orders from idiots. We had a new Lieutenant to lead our sorry asses and ten new replacement soldiers. Our numbers had been depleted as each soldier died. Our platoon was finally up to 14 men again. I was creeping toward the end of my two-year enlistment which would come in October and I was as happy as hell.

Then we received another assignment.

We were assigned to escort refugees into Thailand. The group had been led by prominent men called Tiger Men who led the refugees up the Mekong and over a trail called the Dragon's Back then in to Thailand. It was a long and dangerous trek that skirted Cambodia, Laos and on down to Thailand. We would be assisting a Tiger Man with that dangerous mission.

My new "Louie" (a nickname for Lieutenant) was Joe Briscoe. He was inclined to believe that we were being heroic in leading the refugees, but I thought it would be better if they flew the refugees over ten at a time - but then, whoever listens to a lowly sergeant E6? We're just there to make the dumb decisions work that are made by Military authorities. I guess this was a traditional escape route from Viet Nam, so the refugees agreed with it.

Pao Tang was our Tiger Man; they were called that because each of those men had a tiger tattooed on his back. He had been a doctor in some village to the south. It became quite a parade with our platoon, 25 refugees and a Tiger Man. Our Hmong guide, Chai, commented that we might as well have brought elephants and tanks with us. We were forty plus people making the trek.

We had no trouble until we hit the border of Laos and Cambodia. Then we bumped into a group of men call Pathet Lao. We weren't technically at war with them, but they thought it was fun to extort whatever they could from our group for safe passage. The refugees ponied up any money they had to bribe these little bastards to let us through.

It took us a week to lead the refugees over and through the Dragon's Back and drop them off in Thailand. There we found that some cocky little Military Police rounded up the refugees like cattle and took them to temporary housing. I suppose the MPs were being magnanimous, but they irritated me like a burr under my saddle.

We trekked back the way we had come. It was uneventful until we came to the Dragon's Back. It was a low but craggy set of mountains. The Mekong River burst through the mountain right on the border of Laos and Cambodia.

We had chosen the high mountain trail on the way in to Thailand, but as we were coming back Lieutenant Joe chose the river trail. Well, there is a real problem with the river trail. It follows along the Mekong River, and there are places that are walled on both sides of you. In one of those places we suddenly heard a voice from above yelling at us.

"Su doc toi! Su doc Toi!"

And then someone yelling in English, "We got you Joe! We got you!"

Looking up I could see that the Pathet Lao had us in the neatest crossfire.

Lieutenant Joe said, "Jesus, we're toast!"

"Maybe not," I replied. I turned around to see Willie T. with the whites of his eyeballs big with fear.

"Willie," I said. "You have a better handle on the Viet language than any of us. Can you pop up there and see what they want?"

"I ain't into commitin' suicide this morning, Sarge," Willie T. responded.

"Oh, I don't think it's like that," I conjectured. "I think the little bullies want something we have."

I heard Willie T. give a disgruntled grunt as he said reluctantly, "O.K."

He shouted out something in Vietnamese and then put a white handkerchief on the barrel of his gun. He lifted it up high and then climbed up the cliff face to have a little 'tête-à-tête' with the Pathet Lao leader. About ten minutes later he came back down with a grin on his face,

"Well," I said. "What do they want?"

"He says they will let us go for ten packs of Camels."

"You mean cigarettes?" I said.

"Yep," said Willie T. "Ten packs of Camel cigarettes."

"Can we get ten packs?" I said loudly and began looking around at our men. We came up with nine packs of Camels and one of Winstons.

Willie T. put them in his helmet and crawled back up the cliff. When he returned, he was minus his helmet.

"The little Gooks took my helmet too!" Willie T. exclaimed.

In five minutes, the trail was clear, and we stumbled down it on our way back to Fire Base 6.

No one ever said it, but it was the red-hot command decision of Lieutenant Joe Briscoe that had placed us in that dangerous position. For the rest of that trip all the men kept tight jaws and resentful looks toward our 'Louie.' I thought it odd that a rag tag unit like the Pathet Lao could get us sideways. They must be smart if nothing else.

We knew we were lucky to still be alive.

We slogged on and were about four clicks from Fire Base 6 when we heard gun fire. A.K.'s sounded like a popcorn machine going off.

I said to Lieutenant Joe, "We are coming up on their rear."

"Yeah," he mused. "Go two-by-two. Two on the left rear, two on the right rear."

We put ourselves into formation but stopped in our tracks. Randy, the radio man shouted out, "There's aircraft coming!"

We hunkered down as we heard the slow drone of the C-47's engine. As we raised our heads and looked up, the side door opened and six banks of Vulcan 60'sb, a chain gun that shot 30.06 ammo, cut loose on the Viet Cong that were attacking the base. One pass of the gun and the V.C. who were left standing began running like rabbits – straight at our platoon!

One small VC man and his sister came straight at me.

"No toi! No toi!" He kept shouting. He and I collided. He was on me quicker than I could respond. He reached for my gun; the strap broke and my gun slipped away. I was weaponless except for the small shovel in my pack. I grabbed the handle of it and swung with all my strength. The VC's head leaped from his shoulders; his eyes were blinking in complete surprise. We were both covered in blood.

"Dumb fucking Joe!" His sister screamed at me. "Trying to surrender! Dumb fucking Joe!"

She picked up my rifle and pointed it at me, ready to shoot, then sagged lifeless at my feet. Willie T. had shot her from behind.

Most of the platoon came off with minor wounds but mine was worse. I had just decapitated a 13-year-old boy who was trying to surrender. My whole body shook. The scene of my powerful swing kept flying before my eyes. I felt drained and evil.

'Some sins God will not forgive,' I thought. And this was one of them.'

I was still shaking as Willie T. helped me to camp. Suddenly Captain Granger appeared in front of me and grabbed my hand. "Take these," he said. "It'll help."

I looked down at my hand. There were two tablets with tiny yellow crosses on them - Dexedrine. I got focused real fast after downing them, but the pain of that sinful act has never gone away.

The bombing, euphemistically called a puff, had taken its toll. Over 500 corpses were buried there at Fire Base 6. A big hole was dug, and the bodies were just rolled in. It was the damndest waste of humanity I had ever seen. The country of Viet Nam groaned with me under the pain of war, and it wasn't even half over.

XIV

Hill 543

There had been an increase in the V.C. aggression. It was now supported by the North Vietnamese Army tanks and rockets. We saw more Russian Spetnass too. The Spetnass were the Russian equivalent to our Green Berets. They were deadly.

Captain Granger said, "If it's wearing black and blue, shoot it! We'll sort things out later."

The attacks kept coming with fifty to a hundred men each time, always trying our defenses.

"They are coming from Hill 543!" Granger declared. He was as tired of all the carnage as anyone, maybe more so because he was in command.

"We gotta go into the Zone and take out their base." He told us. "We've done everything from the air, even Napalm, and it won't dislodge them." He shook his head. "It's mano a mano time!"

It was a divisional assault, more than two thousand of our men to take out a heavily fortified NVA base on Hill 543. This was regular Army, spear-headed by Marines. It started with a humorous quirk.

We received an S.O.S. from some Marines who had gotten stuck in an elephant bog.

Elephant bogs are tricky. They look like patches of solid ground covered with little yellow flowers, but the ground is boggy and will suck a man down like quicksand if he gets stuck in it.

Captain Granger singled us out to go on a search and rescue mission.

"Take one of the jeeps," he said. "And go pull them Marines out of the muck!"

We requisitioned a jeep, Big Dick, Willie T. and I, and drove down to where the Marines were. About nine or ten miles south of Firebase 6 there is a great loop of road that skirts the elephant grass bogs. Those Marine recruits had decided to short cut the distance to Firebase 6 by yahooing across the nice even field of little yellow flowers.

There those Marines were, clean shaven with those hundred-pound backpacks still on, waist deep in the bog.

Big Dick yelled out with a bit of glee, "Seems you fellas need a little assistance from the Army!"

We threw each of them a rope and winched them in one at a time with the jeep. They were a thankless and surly lot as they stood on dry land. I never saw anything like it.

"Follow the road," I said. It was hard to keep from laughing at fourteen clean shaven Marines direct from HQ in Nha Trang with mud from the waist down.

"A word of advice," I said, before we left them on the road. "Lose those hundred-pound packs."

A few of them flipped us the bird. The Marines always treated us like we were one step above Charlie, the enemy.

When we arrived back at Firebase 6 there was all sorts of activity happening, choppers coming and going, a tent set up for the brass. It was like dropping into a huge military circus. I and my guys were attached to the 105th Calvary Unit and sent to take Hill 543.

A friend of mine who I knew from Basic Training, Jake Conners, was with the 105th and we briefly had a moment to talk.

"They got you into this mess too?" He said.

"Yeah," I answered. "I don't even know the mission."

"Go up that hill and fuck them up," He said. those are my orders. See you when the shooting's done."

I never saw him again.

We were transported by choppers into what they called an active Landing Zone; that is, people were shooting at us as we exited the aircraft. Our objective was to take and hold as much territory as we could until support units could relieve us. It was nuts!

We linked up with a Turkish unit that was making the way up the hill. Bullets were zinging past us like a swarm of angry bees and now and then someone yelled out in mortal pain, or just collapsed in silence. Death on the battlefield isn't like it's portrayed in the movies. It is quick and sudden.

One of the Turkish soldiers took a round in his left arm, tucked it in his shirt and kept on fighting till he collapsed from loss of blood.

We pushed on up the hill. The rain-soaked mud got into our boots; our hands were caked with blood and grit. Suddenly the enemy started throwing junk at us. It came barreling down the hill. I saw an old desk come bouncing down, the drawers coming out as it bounced. I looked up and suddenly the fins off an old Katusha Rocket bounced down directly in front of me. It hit my left leg and knocked me down. God that hurt! I got up, collected my rifle and led my platoon to the lip of Hill 543.

They were all there, about one hundred fifty NVA, almost out of ammo, but defiant to the end. The Marine Second Battalion came over the hill from the other side.

I turned to give my guys an order and something hit me like a baseball bat on my back, the right side. I lost my wind, and the pain was excruciating. After a few moments I recaptured my wind only to find the Medic leaning over me.

"I don't see any blood," he said. "Let's get this flak vest off of him."

When they peeled of my vest the Medic laughed. "You are one lucky bastard!" he said. He shook my vest in front of me and three slugs fell out, tinkling to the ground.

"You've got three puncture wounds in your right shoulder," he said. "Neosporin and a couple of band aids and you'll be right as rain."

"Jee-zus, Sarge," Willie T. said excitedly. "We thought for sure you bit the big one!"

"Not yet," I said as I pulled myself together. "But damn, my leg hurts!"

"Can you walk on it?" the Medic asked.

I stood up and walked a couple of paces, and said, "It's okay."

Little did I know that it was fractured just below the knee. I didn't have it looked at for three months.

The Marines took a lot of prisoners and my guys were relatively unscathed. Big Dick got hit on the underside of his arm and Gary took a minor hit in his right leg.

The Marines seemed to have it all in hand, so my platoon walked back down to the LZ (Landing Zone). By nightfall we were back at Firebase 6.

I was exhausted. I hit my bunk and was out for nine hours.

The next three days were normal patrol duties until Captain Granger called me into his tent to assign another mission to McCord's Raiders. This time it was to gather information on big VC movements of supplies.

"Do not engage the enemy this time, Egan," the captain said insistently. "I want the information – not your corpse!"

Copters flew us at tree top level into Cambodia. It seemed a very lonely operation. The land was high plains with swampy bogs. We located the VC trail and followed it almost to the Mekong River. We didn't see a soul.

Then we topped a small rise and there, just about three klicks from the river was the most ghastly scene I'd ever witnessed.

It looked like at least thirty thousand corpses lying, rotting in the sun. There was a lonely brown haze over the open grave. The stench was unbearable. Even the carrion birds were only on the edges.

One of my men exclaimed, "Good God Christ!" just before he began throwing up.

It looked like those people had died while trying to flee, mostly women, children and aged.

I announced loudly with the strongest voice I could muster, "Get Gary to call this in." My knees shook and I could not fathom this much inhumanity. My head ached. The images I saw that day have never left me.

Orders came through. "Get the hell out of there! We'll douse it with Napalm."

My whole platoon scurried back over the hill we had just come from and kept retreating. We watched from a distance.

When the A7's planes came over the area there was a ball of flame that shot two or three hundred feet in the air. It must have burned for a full week.

The days dragged on and each day the assault from the NVA grew stronger. The Spetnass added to their strength. We were ordered to shoot any Russian Spetnass we saw, and Captain Granger encouraged us with his decisive orders.

"If these Russians want to stick their toe into this, let's show them what it's really like."

I don't know how many of the Russian soldiers bit the bullet in those days, probably fewer than it seemed, but my crew accounted for twenty-six of them dying. We had to hand it to the Russians. They were well trained and merciless. They were the men who trained the North Vietnamese Army, while we were the trainers of the ARVN, Army of Viet Nam.

Between skirmishes the land dreamed on in silent green peace, especially at dawn. Streams of misty light came through the green jungle like those pictures of heaven you see on post cards and some stained-glass windows. But you knew it would turn into hell at any moment. Only fools or children could appreciate the moments of beauty.

The month of March was ending, and I was exhausted. I was deeply soul-tired of the killing and the senseless slaughter of humanity. I could see no reason or advantage for this war. Was it for oil? Political dominance? The only people who seemed real around us were the whores. They made a living trading their sex for the American soldiers' money and they had no illusions about the rightness of the war. There had been war for them since they had been born and as far as they knew there would be war for their great-grand-children. They survived.

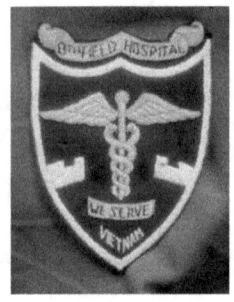

XV

A Dreadful Disease

It was April first, and we were due for the ritual choosing of who would go on furlough. Gary Pasquini who was my B.A.R. (Browning Automatic Rifle) man drew the long match to be the man to go.

"Come on Sarge," he said. "Let's go whoring down in Saigon."

"No Gary," I retorted. "I'm bad luck there." I recalled my sad episode with Left-hand Louie.

"Well, me and Neil will go then," he said. He was happy as a kid at recess.

Neil Snyder was a new member of the platoon. He seemed to me to be gun fodder and poorly trained. We were two men short in our platoon, so we had been assigned to ride protection with the 105th Armored Division.

Neil had been transferred over to us from the 105th because of some insubordination issues. He could pull a trigger, but he had an attitude with everyone. But after he arrived, he felt more at home with our platoon and had taken a liking to Gary. We called it a 'summer school friendship.'

I didn't mind riding on a tank as opposed to walking. My left leg ached most of the time anyway.

We threw cigarette butts and candy wrappers at Gary and Neil as they left for their furlough. We all wished we could go and misbehave a little. But duty called and soon we were in a transport back to Nha Trang. I-Cor and all the tanks were kept in Nha Trang.

The men who drove the tanks we called 'Tankers.' They were an odd lot, patriots to the core and unwavering.

We were assigned to ride on an Abrams tank and do reconnaissance for the Tankers. It was amazing how the Tankers just tore the shit out of the jungle and literally ran civilians over who were tending their rice paddies.

With that outfit we only had one major engagement in a place called Lon Bin. Our guys had taken possession of it seven times, and seven times it was retaken to be inhabited by NVA.

The NVA were determined that Lon Bin would not fall to our troops and they installed an arsenal in the town to defend it. It was strategic to their campaign to reunite all of Viet Nam. To us it was another battle and more bloodshed.

The 105th arrived late and just added weight to a colonel that had already decimated the place. After what seemed a long time the shooting finally stopped. We thought the NVA had pulled back.

As we quietly stood our ground, we saw something odd unfolding. From the east we saw seven brightly dressed Buddhist monks come walking. Their robes were bright yellow. They walked sturdily right across the battlefield as if they didn't have a care in the world.

"They are going to get shot up!" declared

Willie T.

Chai spoke up loudly. "Not so! To harm a monk would be seven different kinds of hell! The NVA will wait until each monk has passed!"

I thought to myself that these powerful monks could end this dust up war in a minute if they chose to.

As soon as the monks had crossed the area the tanks moved in. It was a strongly fortified village that looked like a bombed-out photograph from World War II, Germany. There were only empty shells lying everywhere and craters here and there. In the center of the village was a fountain. A flagpole had been placed in the fountain and on the flagpole a corpse had been hung. The dead man was an NVA colonel that had defended the place; a grizzly reminder to the local population that this was the final time our troops would take Lon Bin.

We didn't fire a shot, which was alright by me. Then my twelve guys were transported by chopper back to Fire Base 6.

Captain Granger greeted us with a long face. He announced, "Seems you are going to be two men short permanently. Pasquini and Snyder picked up a dose of the Black Clap while they were in Saigon. They've been shipped off to an island off the coast of Sri Lanka to rot."

"No!" I said. "So that's it? That can't be! You mean there is no cure?"

Granger continued, "None. And Command has a hard and fast rule about isolation. I'm just informing you of what happened."

To me it seemed that Command might as well have shot them. It was a high price to pay for a little whoring around. I began to hate the Far East with a passion. I swore if I survived this war, I would not set foot in this god forsaken area of the world again.

"One more thing," Captain Granger added. "You and your platoon have a date with the doctors down in Nha Trang for physical exams. They want to make sure none of you guys messed with the whore that got Gary and Neil. The Troop Transport will be here tomorrow."

"Back in Nha Trang," I thought bitterly. "Oh boy."

The choppers came in at 6 a.m. next morning and all twelve of my guys shoved into two Hueys, weapons and all. I wondered if anyone could drive anywhere rather than fly, or if it was safe to do so now. It was a crazy war, in a crazy place, with crazy people all around. We lifted off in a loud whirring, throwing dirt and leaves everywhere.

We settled down on the chopper pad right next to the Med Tent. The medics unceremoniously stripped us and had us each pee in a cup. Then the regimental doctors asked us if we hurt anywhere. I mentioned my leg wound, now old to me but still hurting. I was carted off to X-ray.

The attending doc exclaimed, "Jesus, Soldier! You've been walking on a fractured left leg! How'd this happen?"

"Oh, it was at Hill 543, three months ago," I said. "Old, detached fins off a rocket flew down a hill and hit me."

"Well, you're goddamned tough," he said. You've got an S fracture just under the left knee. It'll heal okay, but you're going to have trouble with it later in life."

"Thanks," I replied. He dismissed me.

The docs decreed that all twelve of our platoon were fit to fight except our radio man, Randy.

He had a cold. They pumped him full of penicillin, patted his bottom where it hurt and sent him out to be shot at again.

XVI

Tet

Months moved slowly for us at Fire Base 6. We now had a dull knowledge of the 8-kilometer radius of the place. Daily we walked our way through, cleaning out the new jungle growth with machetes, scanning for the enemy, counting out the clicks.

A small village named Con Lai was nearby. Sometimes a few of the women from the village brought us food. There was one old lady, I could not estimate her age, but her face was full of wrinkles and she had no teeth. She spoke the best English. She told us it was her duty to make sure we didn't starve. I suspect she had tasted our MRE's (meals ready to eat) and wanted to trade. She called us lads.

By now we had erected a mobile kitchen of sorts. We called the old woman Sadie, and she brought her five Amer-Asian daughters to cook for us. They, like most of the women in Viet Nam, were either very beautiful or very homely. There was no in-between.

Each day they came over to Fire Base 6 with the tastiest but strangest, unidentified, food. They also for ten American dollars, would take you into your yurt and let you have your way with them.

It was, for us soldiers, a pleasant time, and the Viet Cong kept their distance and we kept ours.

Then it was the season of Tet. It was the end of March 1969 as the rains began. It was as though someone in the heavens was pouring water on us out of a huge jug. The days were warming, many days were near one hundred degrees, still pouring down rain. This is when this beautiful green land became horrible and stifling.

Even the monkeys that usually hooted in the trees all hunkered down. The amount of water falling from the sky was unimaginable to me.

During this intolerable time is when the North Vietnamese Army chose to make its push. Tet is the Vietnamese New Year, and this part of the war became the Tet Offensive. Now we had to keep our wits as we defended our position.

The NVA pushed hard against Fire Base 6, forcing us to retreat backward past Con Lai.

There was a Russian tank sitting in the middle of Sadie's improvised kitchen we had built as we pulled back from the hill. We could hear the dull thud of bombs being dropped by B-52's and jets screaming through rattling bursts of machine gun fire.

It was then some desk jerk ordered us back to Nha Trang. We were carried by choppers out of there and back to the big base. The whisper was that we were getting ready to invade Cambodia.

Either fortune or someone's idiot move kept me from that grand enterprise. We were in the locker room behind the 82nd Army's Fire Base. There were Quonset huts placed there that had been drug out on the old runway for personnel to bunk in while at the base.

As usual our platoon boys were cleaning their ordinance and joking around. I was exhausted as I sat there. I was thinking we were lucky to be pulled out of the fray where we'd been up north.

Willie T. was jerking the eject on his M-16 and saying, "Goddamned piece of shit!" when suddenly the shell in the chamber discharged.

I felt a growing pain in my left hip and saw blood gushing from the wound.

"Oh, Christ!" Willie T. screamed. I passed out right there, and when I woke up, I was looking at a beautiful nurse looking dreamily into my face.

She was saying, "I think he's coming around."

I could tell I was under the influence of a lot of morphine. When I was able, I pulled back the sheet and could only see a thumbnail sized hole in the side of my butt, and my whole left side turning black and blue.

Now the thin, pale white doctor was sitting in front of me.

"You're one lucky soldier," he said. "We got the bullet out and it was only inches from your renal artery."

I asked hopefully, "Will this send me home?"

"No. Probably not," the doctor said. "Can you walk?"

I got up, not able to stand up straight. My whole left side ached.

"Jeez," I exclaimed. "Getting shot hurts worse than any beating I ever had. What happened?"

Willie T. was there beside me too and said, "I was trying to get a spent shell out of that damned gun of mine. Well, it wasn't spent, and it went off. They say it ricocheted on three metal lockers before it hit you. I'm a damned fool!" At that moment I tended to agree with him.

My injury kept our platoon in reserve, and it was two weeks before I could hobble out on the battlefield again. The planes kept coming in with news of the defeats of the ARVN – Army of Viet Nam. They were supposed to be backing up our troops, but they broke and ran, leaving the Marines to face the music.

Politics raged on too. We watched T.V. news from Saigon showing monks setting themselves on fire in protest to one thing or another to do with the war. From the look of things, I was again sure the world had gone crazy. Why couldn't we leave these people alone to have their own civil war. Why were we there anyway? But I was a lowly E6, a sergeant, and everything moved on orders.

While we were at Nha Trang some of the Biggies came to talk to us troops. We all had to stand to attention when General Westmoreland came.

He said, "The North is losing its power to make war... and they cower in fear at our superior weapons and tactics."

I never heard a crowd laugh so loud at his statement. That man had no knowledge of the Asian mind. These people were upset when their troops died and went to meet Buddha, but not overly disturbed. When any Vietnamese bit it, those who remained living, danced a little jig, knowing that the dead men's women, rice and prized possessions would be divvied up among them.

They did not fear us and the piece of junk we were given to fight with reinforced that we were not a menace to them. Most of our men had procured one of the enemy's A.K. and ammunition – something to shoot with when your M16 froze up on you. The A.K. 47 could shoot even with mud in the barrel. It was much slower but effective in taking the enemy out.

We soldiers who were fighting this war called it the "Great Eastern Farce." The only thing that was real about it was death and the occasional good whore.

Everyone cheated out there, especially the government – ours and theirs. I even knew a supply sergeant who bragged to me that he sent an entire Huey Helicopter home, in parts.

While I was healing from my wound, I got a letter from Command.

"You have been awarded the Purple Heart pursuant to the recommendation of your commander, Gerald B. Hensley."

"Christ," I thought. "I was shot accidentally. I went to see Gerald B. Hensley, a captain fresh out of the Academy and I asked him, "Why did I receive this?"

"You were shot," he explained. "It was on foreign soil. You get a Purple Heart. Anything else, soldier.?"

The Army obviously did not operate on Military Intelligence. In this situation they don't give you more than one Purple Heart. If you've received one and have another wound, you get a paper certificate. They gave me this paper saying I get another award, my second.

In a couple of weeks, they reassigned me to my old platoon. The boys were tickled that I was back, and we could go after the North Vietnamese Army together.

"Let's wait and see," I said. "Uncle Sugar may have a dreadful surprise for us."

It turned out my statement was pure truth. We'd been hooked into the invasion of Cambodia, and since we'd been there before, we were again assigned to support the Green Berets that were making trouble over there. All I knew about Cambodia was that they had pretty women and very mean men. The Mekong was wet, muddy and full of Caiman Crocodiles that didn't mind dragging an occasional human into his underwater lair.

Cambodia was not at war with us, so why start trouble?

It was June 1969. The dry season was just beginning. We still had an occasional downpour, but by and large the violent thunderstorms and sheet lightning were gone. The season of Tet was ending.

Now we were three kilometers from the 105th when it happened.

Someone yelled "Get down!" and then someone, I thought it was Babe Ruth, hit me in the head with his Louisville Slugger. My mind wandered in a grey haze. I was calling for someone, but I can't remember who. I wandered in the greyness until some asshole was screaming at me - "Wake up!"

How dare they. This grey area was very comfortable. I had no pain. Suddenly there was a flash of light and the terrified face of Willie T. Devoy was spitting out excited words over me.

"Oh Christ! Oh Christ!" he said. "They shot him in the head!"

I had trouble opening my left eye and there was blood everywhere I was able to look. It was my blood.

The Corpsmen came and I was lifted up bodily and placed in a chopper. The men surrounding me were a concerned lot and every time I tried to sit up and speak, they held me down. I wondered that they hadn't even taken my helmet off. I tried to use my senses. Toes worked; fingers worked; eyes worked. But I could only open the left one a bit.

Someone asked me, "Do you know your name?"

"John Egan," I replied.

"Rank?"

"E6."

"Where were you born?"

"He's with us!" yelled one of the Corpsmen.

All those men around me cheered!

I asked the Corpsman, "Can I get this can off my head?"

"Not just now," he said. "When we get to Nha Trang."

I was awake enough to know better than to argue with a Corpsman. When you are wounded, they all appear as though they are generals, and no insubordination is tolerated.

I tried to relax but there was a high buzzing in my ears. I went in and out of consciousness and dreamed of my girl-friend Karen. She was so close to me. Her skin was soft. Her hair was long and clean. I was about to reach up and touch her beautiful breast when some damned fool kept hammering on the bedroom door, yelling, "Stop fucking my wife!" End of dream.

I awoke with a team of doctors and nurses fussing over me. They stood around me like a jury dressed in white, trying to decide if I was going to live or die.

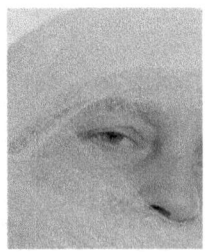

I'd been there for three or four days and I'd been unconscious much of the time. My head was in a massive bandage and I was wondering if I'd been maimed for life. Just then, who should walk into the room but Captain Granger. He smiled and saluted me.

"Looks like you took another one for the team," he said. "The good news is, you're out of here. You're going home."

"What's the glitch," I asked.

He laughed. "You've been in this man's army too long," he said.

"I don't know but there's bound to be a curve in the road ahead," I said. "There always is."

Captain Granger added, "They tell me you didn't exactly get hit in the head."

"Yeah," I replied. I had heard the doctors talking about my injury. Lucky or not, the damned bullet caught me between the helmet and the liner. It drove a piece of the liner into my head and then ricocheted out. I guess I'll live to tell the story." I laughed. It hurt.

I asked him, "What about you? You look all Marine Corps. What's up?"

"I'm on my way home too," he said.

"You gonna take your little woman home too?" I asked.

A look of sadness came over his face as he said, "No, she was killed the night they over ran the base."

He fell silent, saluted me, then turned on his heel and left.

I guess he really loved that little woman who fussed around and saw to his every need. War doesn't paint a pretty picture, not like the romantic pictures we'd seen about WWII. I suppose it's got to be a clear win or lose proposition for people to move on and return to normality.

But what am I saying? No one ever wins a war.

My head began to ache again. It was time for another nap.

I spent two weeks at the Nha Trang Medical unit and my head healed up so all you could see was a one-inch scar close to the crown of my head. My bruised face came back into focus as the swelling left, and the earlier accidental wound in my hip caused me a bit of pain and a limp. I was in fine form.

Now I had time on my hands before I could get back to the States. I had contacted Mai Li, my friend Louie's girl, after he had been killed. I had written to her twice to let her know what had happened to Louie and then again trying to console her. One day she drove up from Saigon to show me around. She being a stewardess had given her perks.

She could check out one of the Air Tai cars for business or pleasure any time she was free.

We drove around and talked. I was amazed when she told me she'd been invited to the U.S. by Louie's parents.

"It seems you would have moved on," I said.

She shrugged her shoulders and said, "I got my needs, but no one will ever replace him."

We drove on in silence.

"Maybe I will just go to the States and stay," she said. "This land has no more color for me. Yes, I think I will."

I could see a small tear gather at the corner of her eye. I felt helpless in that moment, unable to comfort her.

Mai Li was a wonderful girl. She was sweet, sexy and sharp as a tack. She asked me if I wanted to make love to her; somehow, I couldn't bring myself to do that. I remembered poor Louie. It didn't seem the right thing to do. When she dropped me back at the Nha Trang base she smiled and said good-bye with the best kiss I'd ever had.

"See you in the states," she laughed.

XVII

Back To The Good Old U.S.A.

Now it was time to tend to business. I needed a large jet to get me out of Viet Nam. I was told the next Troop Transport would be in two weeks, but for me that wasn't acceptable. I needed to get out of there quickly. I finally was able to get a commercial flight out of Saigon headed east to Istanbul. I was to report to Fort Benning for new training for my "traumatic brain injuries," but more pressing was the feeling I needed to get out of the war zone.

"Anywhere but here," I thought.

It was strange that I had to beg and borrow two thousand dollars from a friend at Nha Trang to get air fare and traveling money. He was a Supply Sergeant and had money to spare. I was pretty sure he had made his fortune doing black market deals to the States.

I got on a British jet, BOAC, and found it was not quite the luxury liner the Americans were used to. It was a long and arduous flight. I slept a good deal of the time and dreams came to me of things that happened to me in Nam. The most vivid dream was the time my platoon fell ill with the dengue fever. I smiled at the memory, but it was an awful time. We all sweated and peed all day long for three days. We were as weak as lambs. Regimental sent some doctors to us up from Nha Trang who poked us full of some medicine that stopped the loss of fluids we were experiencing. The doctors pronounced it a "mild case." God help those who got the real thing!

At the time if the NVA had known how sick we were they could have taken our base without a shot.

One of our guys, Bill Martins, was so weak he fell into the slit trench we had dug and used for toileting. Strange to me was the thing that came to mind as I traveled away from it all.

Scenes of battles and death shot through my mind and made me toss and turn in my seat. I awoke to the friendly face of a stewardess saying, "We're about to land in New Delhi to refuel, sir."

My eyes were barely open and looking at her, when she said, "Perhaps you would like to get out and stretch your legs before we continue to Istanbul."

She smiled at me with a secret suggestive look and said, "My name us Jeanette, sir. I hope you're doing okay."

She was the most beautiful woman I had seen since I had visited with Mai Li in Saigon. Her Raven black hair was twisted into a bun at the nape of her neck. As I studied her beautiful eyes my mind took a different turn and I imagined what the stewardess and I could accomplish together. I was coming out of three years of celibacy and my body ached to end it.

The airliner set down gently in New Delhi and I got out to look around.

There were more people here than in Bangkok. They were crowded together like cord wood, back to front. I began to yearn for more deserted places in the world. I had been in a crowded and destitute country for too long.

A beggar held out his hand. He looked as though he lived right there on the curb in the airport. I put a few coins in his hand and suddenly a policeman hailed me.

"Please do not indulge the untouchables, sir," he said. "They will follow you for alms and make your stay here most unpleasant."

I wrinkled my brow and wondered how a civilization such as this had survived.

I turned and walked back to the plane. I was so tired of this kind of crap. Their poverty was not just overbearing, it was over whelming. Why couldn't men treat one another as equals?

I was glad to resettle in my seat and the beautiful stewardess came by to check whether our seatbelts were on.

"I hope you enjoyed your stay in New Delhi," she said with a smile. I smiled back at her with her perfect figure and imagined her without her clothing.

There was a roar, a rush of the engines and a jolt, as the airplane became airborne again. My mind turned from my fantasy as I looked out at the landscape of New Delhi shrinking to a size so you could see where the city stopped, and the country began.

Clouds gathered and soon we were cruising above them. I felt like I was lifted away in a heavenly bird. All sense of speed and flight ceased. The sky was pale blue and the clouds slate grey. The plane seemed to just hang there motionless.

I knew we were going a good four hundred miles an hour, but the illusion of motionless flight was so real.

Another five hours passed, and the sweet voice of the lovely stewardess came over the intercom saying, "In thirty minutes we will be landing in Istanbul. Please make sure you have all your carry-on luggage you brought with you. Thank you."

We touched down gently and taxied to the loading area. I remembered the gentle touch downs because of the difference in the way we had traveled by Huey's and had been set down rapidly and roughly wherever we went in Nam. Now the doors opened, and I stepped into the bright dry sun of Istanbul.

The clerk at the airport ticket office told me I had two days before there was a BOAC flight to London. I was in no hurry, so I thanked him and went in search of a place to stay.

Just ten blocks from the terminal stood the Istanbul Hilton, bright, new and welcoming. Ninety-four bucks a night for a double bed. I booked two days and went to room 204, shed my clothes, hit the bed and was asleep before my head touched the pillow.

We had arrived in the morning. Now it was approaching six-thirty and the sun was setting. A knock came at my door.

"Yes," I said, and reached for my gun. Old habits die hard.

"Mr. Egan, this is Jeanette, from the plane."

Good Lord, I thought. Am I dreaming? Are my dreams about to come true? I opened the door and there she stood, as beautiful as the sunrise.

Her lovely voice said, "I hope you don't mind. I was just concerned about you."

I held the door wide open and she slipped into the room. She wasted no time. Her dress fell from her and in a few moments, we were entwined in the large warm bed.

She was at once tender and passionate. I'd never been with a woman who knew as much about making love.

"You seemed so alone," she whispered. "My heart beat faster just to see you smile."

"How did you know where I'd be?" I asked.

"A sneaky trick," she smiled. "I asked the luggage boy where they'd sent your bags."

"I didn't know I was that easy to track," I said. "It doesn't matter now. I'm so glad you found me."

Jeanette was beautiful and had smooth olive skin. It felt so good to be with her. I could have stayed with her forever, but in the morning, she was up and busy.

"I've got a flight back to Saigon this morning," she informed me. "I won't be back for three days." Her lower lip quivered, and her proud eyes dropped.

She whispered back to me, "You're the best lover I've ever had. Take care of yourself."

Then she slipped out the door and I never saw her again. I should have followed her, chased her down and begged her to marry me, but I didn't. Damn, I didn't.

Alone in Istanbul I fell prey to one of the many tours they offered. Small dark men with red fez hats barked up business at the airports, trying to snatch rich tourists. One man held up a sign that looked so American – "Casey's Tours" in three languages, English, French and Greek - Arabic script below the larger words were on a big yellow and red sign.

I saw an airplane headed east and the thought of sweet Jeanette flashed through my mind. Five-foot-four inches, olive skin, dark brown eyes, black hair. I felt a twinge of remorse again. Ah well, it would be a fool's errand to let my mind keep running after her.

The small man with the red fez hat kept jabbering about the great Roman Emperor Constantine and how he separated from the Western Empire in 300 something A.D. It was all very interesting. We were standing under a great cliff on a cement dock. Suddenly there was a sound as if someone had thrown a large ripe melon off the cliff right at us. A well-dressed British woman began to scream. There was blood all over her white and blue polka dot dress.

The man in the red fez broke into Arabic and shook his fist at the cliff. Apparently, someone had thrown a man off the Ankara from three hundred feet above us and there he lay, his vital fluids leaking from him all over the dock. The poor British woman fainted as a group of policemen showed up also babbling in Arabic. They whisked the body away.

It was ghastly and I had thought I'd left all that behind in Viet Nam. The event numbed my brain and made ordinary people run for cover.

It turned out he was a thief and had fallen behind in his guild payments. The guild did not take kindly to their dead beats.

The ride back to the Istanbul Hilton was silent with people hanging their heads in grief for the poor dead soul. I think it was shock we were all in. it brought back the harshness of combat to me. It was impossible to shake the fear.

A fire fight lasts about twenty minutes. In that twenty minutes men lose their lives. All one can do is advance or retreat and try not to look at all the blood and mayhem that occurs. The memory of those events never goes away.

Your hands shake, you want to piss your pants, run away but you don't. There are no atheists in foxholes because each person is hoping and praying hard that the next death will not be his own. Every death you witness brings it back to focus on your own death and you want to throw up. The memory of violent death is solid in your soul.

The bus swung into the parking lot of the Istanbul Hilton with just enough time to pack our carry-ons and get into the shuttle for the B.O.A.C. flight to London.

I was shuffled into a seat and within forty-five minutes we were airborne. I asked for three mini bottles of Seagram V.O. and I was ready for a long inflight nap. The scene of the man hitting the cement dock kept playing and replaying in my head. I slept but could not forget.

I awoke to the friendly face of a different stewardess telling me we were fifteen minutes from Heath Row, London. Half the world had slipped away from me as I slept.

It was a quick transition to a TWA flight to Kennedy Airport and again I passed out. I awoke this time to the dark night whistling past. I wondered about my friends Willie T., Big Dick, and Gary. I knew Gary was in for a long painful death, but not just yet. He was spending the rest of his days on an island off the coast of Sri Lanka with the other people who had contracted Black Syphilis.

I knew Willie T. would get along okay, and so would Big Dick, if he kept clear of the Saigon whores. Their time in Nam would be up soon and they'd be back in the U.S.A.

From then on, the flight became boring. I read a magazine called Elle to fill the time. Soon a magnificent sunrise appeared on the port side of the plane and the pilot's squeaky intercom said, "Back in the U.S.A. folks, twenty-five minutes until departure."

The rose-colored morning spread, and the sun's first arc stabbed light over the ocean. I felt I was home. I'd been gone for what felt like an eternity.

I had forgotten how fast people move about in the U.S.A. When I got off the plane, I was whisked away to a waiting lounge by two chatty Black girls. They were listening to James Brown on a boom box. A funny little man dressed in a blue uniform came into the lounge shouting, "All flights to the West Coast at Dock 724!"

I was travel weary and needed to rest. When I boarded the TWA bound for San Francisco it seemed like the last lap of a long race. It was another eight hours before I finally looked out the window to see the Golden Gate and the bright sun setting on the Pacific Ocean. I let out a sigh. I was home.

XVII

T.B.I.

Traumatic Brain Injury

A Muni bus took me into the city from the
airport. Just off the tarmac there was a collection of
teen-aged girls, all different sizes and faces. I was
dressed in my Army uniform, the only clothes I had.
They spit at me and screamed. They kept calling me,
"Baby Killer!" It was strange for me, a shock to my
physical being. I was proud of my service to the
Army and my country, but these young women filled
the atmosphere with their hatred and disgust.

I got off the bus at Civic Center and walked
down Eddy Street to Tina's Café. In the days before
I was in the service it was a good place to have
dinner. Across the cul de sac was the "Drug-free
Park." There were kids and junkies there, shooting
up and leaving their drug paraphernalia around.

I noticed a little Black girl riding her bike around in the cul de sac. She looked to be about nine years old. As she passed the alleyway between the park and the old Jefferson Hotel a man reached out and grabbed her. He pulled her into the alley and was pulling her pants down with the intention of raping her. The fire in me rose. I ran to the alley, grabbed a garbage can lid and slammed him straight in the face. I yelled at the girl, "Run!" and she did, at the same time screaming for her mother.

I kept hitting the man who was yelling at me, "Enough! Enough!" I hit him hard one more time in the face and he fell to the ground and lay still.

I stood over him and realized what I'd just done. I was thinking, "Good Lord! There will be some brig time in this for me."

About then a policeman arrived. A tall level-eyed sergeant arrived and looked me up and down. He very quietly said to me, "You were never here. Understand me? I'll give you five minutes to be somewhere else. Now Git!"

I ran around the block then up to Van Ness and over to the In and Out Burger joint. Nothing was ever said about the incident. I went in and ordered a meal and sat down.

When I came out someone hailed me. "Hey, Johnny!" a guy said. "What are you doing down here?"

It was a man we called Old Joe, a friend from my hometown, Eureka. He had been the dock manager on the waterfront in Eureka when I was a kid.

He'd caught me and my friend Richard back then, starting a fire to the dock on the bay. To us he was hell on wheels and scared us to death. He had punished us for our misdeed. First, he made us work at one of the fisheries, pushing fish guts off the dock for a few hours. Next, he fed us and lectured us about how the docks were so expensive to build. Richard managed to escape him as soon as he could, but I liked the man. I hung around and Old Joe became my friend and mentor for a long time.

Now Old Joe said to me, "I see you've been in the service."

"Yeah," I responded. "I just got back into town."

He looked me over like a dad looking over a son.

"Been in a fight, huh?"

"It's a long story," I said.

"Well, you got a place to stay yet?"

I responded, "No, I just hit town."

He reached into his shirt pocket and pulled out some keys.

"Number 3 Bay Street," he said. "It's empty right now." He put the keys in my hand then asked me if I'd eaten.

"Just at the In and Out," I said.

"That's no meal," he said. "Get yourself on down to Original Joe's and tell them it's on me, then get yourself up to 3 Bay Street and get some rest."

He smiled that easy smile I'd always known and said, "Glad you made it back in one piece."

He added, "There's a car there. That silver key on the ring. You use it."

"I don't know what to say, Joe," I said.

"It's doing my part," he said, "for the guys I know."

He turned on his heel and began whistling down Van Ness Avenue.

I hopped the bus to Aquatic Park and went on over to Bay Street. Number three was one of those units of semi-detached houses that clustered on Bay and Embarcadero. I'd wait till later for dinner at Original Joe's.

I opened the door and found it was 1970's luxury furnishings inside. I hit the sheets and passed out for more than ten hours.

I awoke feeling my exhaustion was over and knew I had a date to keep at Travis Airfield. TBI

Therapy. Traumatic brain injury. I was to report to a Lieutenant Alexander at 10 o'clock in the morning. My head hurt and my left eye kept going into spasms. But otherwise I felt fine. I thought about using the car but when I saw it was a 1970's black Lincoln it seemed a bit much to show up to the Airfield that way.

There was work going on for the beginnings of the Bart (Bay Area Transit system) at that time. Regular transit then was still a bus out of Seventh Street Station. It was so crowded I had difficulty finding the bus to Travis. It was running eleven minutes late. By the time I was dumped off at the gate four MP's escorted me to a large portable building. When I entered there were about twenty other guys standing next to the most gorgeous blonde woman. She had single bars on her shoulders – she was Lieutenant A. Alexander. What a woman! She was about five foot eight inches tall and her long blonde hair was done up in a tight bun. Her eyes were piercing blue and her figure was the finest I'd ever seen. She could have been a movie star. But when she spoke, she was all Army.

"Now that Mr. Egan has chosen to join our group we can get started," she said. She was very serious and started by introducing herself.

"My name is Lieutenant Aileen Alexander."

She then went on to describe our collective injuries and finished with, "And that's why we are here, to learn how to cope in civilian society for each of you and your particular injury."

She droned on for some time and then strongly stated one important thing.

"You must talk about it," she said. "I don't care how horrible a thing you think it was, but you must talk about it!"

She continued, "It's true, civilians won't understand. They may be horrified. They may think you are full of shit. But it is not for them to judge. It is for you to get your story out, to testify to your bravery or cowardness. You will find that by telling it, it will be less heavy on you. Learn how to cry – let it out!"

There were whispers around the room and someone was heard to say distinctly, "She's full of shit!"

We were sitting all around her. We began speaking in a clockwise manner. Bowgen, a big Native American man made a stumbling attempt, then Zack, a small wiry man with his bandage still on his head. He wept as he spoke about little children catching fire from a Napalm drop. Soon it came around to my turn and I blurted out, "There are some sins God will not forgive."

I spoke about the decapitation of the young Vietnamese boy I had mistakenly killed in the middle of battle. There was silence when I was done, and tears were in many eyes. The story of John Egan wasn't new to them. They had all lived it and I was convinced the blame lay firmly on the U.S. Military and the U.S. Government with its continual quest for power and oil.

Day after day of this group therapy continued. I and the boys got better at telling the tale of our ongoing nightmares. Six weeks passed and the Traumatic Brain Injury counseling was over.

It was on a Saturday morning a couple of weeks later when there came a knock on the door. It was Lieutenant Aileen Alexander. I saluted her, more out of habit than anything else.

"At ease, soldier," she said softly. "I just came around to see how you're adjusting to civilian life. She looked around the flat Old Joe had given me, Number 3, Bay Street.

She shook her head and said, "It seems you're doing quite well."

"Oh," I said. "This place. I can explain. It's on loan from an old friend of mine."

"Pretty good friend, I'd say." She lowered her voice and continued. "I need to tell you, being the higher rank I am, I don't have much of an opportunity for, you know…love."

She stepped into the living room and I shut the door behind her. I watched as she kicked off her shoes and settle on the couch. She loosened her Army tie and popped the button on her pants.

"I was wondering, Mr. Egan, if you would make love to me." She moistened her lips with her pink tongue. It was an invitation I couldn't refuse.

When we were finished with making love, she lit a cigarette and sighed deeply.

"I think you're ready to meet the outside world, John," she said.

She dressed carefully then walked out the door. I never saw or heard from her again.

XVIII

Recovery

I took to hanging out at Aquatic Park with all the old Chinese men. They didn't speak much English and looked at me with silent contempt. I returned their gaze with just as much contempt and we were okay with that relationship. I received notice in the mail with my last paycheck from the Army. The letter congratulated me for successfully completing the Traumatic Brain Injury Training. They also thanked me for my service. Thus, I thought that was a back-handed (unofficial) discharge. I was angry. I was angry at the goddamned Army for jerking me out of a perfectly good seventeen and three quarter years of existence and putting me squarely in the mouth of hell, in danger of death every moment, then laughing and putting me back on the civilian shelf. Thank you for your service my ass.

Thinking I was already released from the military, I shed my uniform as soon as I had reached the Bay area.

It was time I went back to see my parents. My dad I knew at least would be proud of me as his son. I took the bus to Santa Rosa, then got off and hitched my way back to Eureka, my hometown. I was born and raised there behind what is popularly called the Redwood Curtain. Eureka is a small town one hundred miles south of the Oregon border. It is isolated, rural, and deliciously dull. Like most small towns it has only two industries, there it is fishing and the timber industry, and more currently, has lost a lot of its timber companies.

My last ride was with an opinionated hippie. As he dropped me off, I took a deep breath of the fresh air of Eureka. I coughed and almost choked to death! While I'd been gone, they had put up a pulp mill which was spewing out acidic exhaust. This was not the Eureka I knew.

I made my way, duffle bag and all to the family home near Eureka High School. I went 'round the back and poked my head into the kitchen.

"Hello!" I shouted. "Is anybody home?"

My mother came out of the bedroom with a surprised look and was all over me in a second. Dad was out in the garage. He came in to see what all the ruckus was. My brother was up the street with his friend Randy.

I was home, but things had changed. I was changed. I was not the hopeful teenager who had already been making a name as a musician. I was not the hopeful kid who'd been packed off to the war. I was a used soul full of anger and contempt. My father looked hard at me and said, "You've been through a lot son. Settle down here, get a job, get a wife and buy a house. The anger will go away."

I looked him in the eye, no longer in the father and son relationship. We were two old men, knowing too damn much and just trying to cope.

"Let me think on that, Dad," I said.

I spent my time at the Captain's Galley, the local watering hole. I drank too much, and bull shitted with other veterans. Bloody Mary's were fifty cents each and I drank my share.

One day a particularly vocal man came into the bar. He was a disabled Veteran and a war protester. He'd lost his legs in his years in Viet Nam. You know the kind, he carried hand printed signs and yelled obscenities if the police got close. He was as angry as I was.

He was organizing an anti-war protest that he said would go to Washington D.C. He had a big yellow school bus that he said was going to go back and blockade the Whitehouse. His name was Don McKenzie. He seemed very interested in me once he found out I was a recipient of the purple heart. "What a statement," he said, "when even a wounded veteran throws his medals over the wall at the Whitehouse. You are made for this," he said.

In my anger and frustration, I agreed with him. A stand up should be made; I would be a true patriot! Historic consequences could be made, like Patrick Henry in the Revolutionary War had said, "Give me Liberty or give me death!"

"Hah!"

He said we'd be gone two weeks; I had nothing better to do so I joined the group. He had gathered several people as disgruntled as I was. We all chipped in for the gas and food, all twelve of us. As we went through small towns the news followed us.

In every town we picked up people, mostly Vets, opposed to the war. Don's 'Merry Raiders' filled the bus and swelled to about forty people. We even picked up a girl named Tina. She seemed more interested in getting close to every man on board.

The vet sitting behind me poked me and said, "Hey, we're in a sexual revolution!"

"How's that?" I asked.

"While we were in Nam, they took out all the stops!"

I laughed. "No kidding."

Tina coaxed men to have sex with her in the back of the bus. Nearly half the men spent time with her. She saw it as her duty to keep the men's spirits high.

A week later we arrived in Washington D.C. to join the throngs of people that protested in front of the Whitehouse. Many people threw garbage over the fence and screamed and yelled. There were altercations with the police; it was a bedlam of protest.

There were several buses that unloaded people at one time. There was a lot of confusion. Then it was the Veterans turn. There were placards with "STOP THE WAR!" and "VETERANS STOPPING THE WAR." The Vets who were protesting pushed their way to the fence and began throwing their medals over it. I was shouting "End the War! End the War!" I was one of only three Vets discarding Purple Heart Medals. I was so angry I felt inspired as I threw the medal and four certificates over the fence. Then, as I was screaming and had done the deed, I looked up and noticed all the cameras blinking at us and I got a sick uneasy feeling in my stomach.

The police moved in to stop us, but even they were no match for Vets who were freshly discharged and didn't give a damn. I had picked up two large signs, waving one in each hand. One said, "Stop this insane war you Idiot!" and "We've given our all for the U.S.A.!"

It was insane and the only thing missing was the bullets whizzing past my head. A big Black guy who'd been a Master Sergeant named Marvin was clubbed by a policeman. I remember the sound of his body being hit- it sounded like the thuds of blows to an old Oak tree, but then he took the stick away from the policeman and rendered a blow to the cop that broke his arm and rendered him unconscious. Marvin's probably still in jail for that one.

Tina appeared next to the fallen policeman, pulled down her pants and squatted over the man's head and pissed on him.

With that I began to back away from the crowd. My anger was starting to lose its color and I realized this action was not going to change anything to the good. I wondered what the hell I was doing.

The newsmen descended on Don McKenzie like a hoard of flies. I'd seen so many people in war get wounded and killed and this was a repeat of the hell I'd been through. The whole world again seemed insane.

I walked away from the demonstration and toward the Washington D.C. Train Station. I located what we used to call a Night Flyer train that went coast to coast for $200. I booked a sleeper car to the West Coast. I was done expressing my opinion to the world. It knew it didn't change a damned thing and left me feeling helpless and empty.

After I'd paid for the train fare, I realized I had only two hundred dollars left before I was dead broke. What I needed now was a job.

I still had the keys to Number 3 Bay Street in San Francisco, so I had a place to go. Old Joe would have a job for me. He always did. He was like family to me.

My sleeper was next to a car full of teen-agers, all about 17 years old. I was only twenty by then, but I felt old beyond reckoning. I tried to sleep but the sound of gunfire kept jolting me awake. I kept a loaded .45 caliber Colt automatic under my pillow - just in case the bad dreams turned back into reality and I found myself back at Firebase 6. It was silly but it made me feel better.

The young people in the next car were partying and one cute girl swung into my sleeper.

"Dennis is after me," she said. "Can I hide in here in your sleeper?"

I was sitting on the lower bench and motioned to the opposite seat, but she swung up into my upper berth and got under the covers.

"You could join me," she whispered.

I thought I had nothing to lose so I replied, "Why not?" and swung up into the bunk with her.

There wasn't much about sex this girl didn't know. She was a typical middle-class hippie and acted as though she'd been exploring the avenue since she was thirteen.

"My name is Donna," she said. "What's yours?"

But she seemed so unbearably innocent it was hard making love to her without feeling like I might be molesting a child. But then, by her actions, I could tell she knew exactly what to do.

Donna stayed with me until we reached Oakland. She wanted me to tell her all about the war. Her favorite word to use was "really," which she used over and over.

I told her about how Louie had died and all the other grisly events. At each telling she responded to me with that "Really." When we arrived at the station in Oakland she jumped up, kissed me and said, "I gotta split. My mom and dad are picking me up."

I wasn't surprised. She probably had to get back to her high school classes. She was in love with love, no meaning beyond that.

I took the Muni transport back to #3 Bay Street. It was just as I had left it.

I was preparing to go out to dinner at a nearby Chinese restaurant when a knock come on the door. I spoke through the door saying, "Yes?"

"We are looking for Mr. John Egan. FBI."

I opened the door and two men in dark suits and wearing sunglasses stood there, their feet apart, looking intimidating. They waved a warrant for my arrest in my face.

They introduced themselves as Agents Fred White and Alan Dickee.

"Why am I being arrested?" I asked.

"The warrant says you are AWOL," Mr. White stated. "We will give you time to shave and dress in your uniform." I had the sense that if I didn't comply with their wishes, they would do it for me, in other words, it was an order.

"I can't be AWOL," I responded. "I just finished Traumatic Brain Injury training."

"Well, bring your documentation with you," Mr. White said. "We'll straighten this out downtown."

XIX

Arrested

The two Federal Agents took me to the Federal Building down by U.N. Plaza. I had grabbed my papers about completion of my Traumatic Brain Injury Program and the letter stating that my check would be the last one from the Military. It didn't seem to matter. I was in custody.

The one thing that was abundantly clear was, other than my being AWOL as they said, they hadn't charged me with anything.

Soon it became clearer that I was being detained by a higher power. Three hours into my arrest and detainment, two Military Police entered my room.

"We've been instructed to take the prisoner to the Presidio," said the tall, thin straight soldier.

I've always thought MPs were wonderful, full of duty and righteousness.

"Sergeant," he addressed me emphatically.

"What's this all about?" I asked.

"General Broward requests your presence, sir."

"The Brass, huh?" I said.

I was hustled out the back door of the building, so to speak, and put in an Army Transport. It took twenty minutes to arrive at the Presidio. Everyone around me was in a very somber mood, like I'd tried to assassinate the President or some other drastic thing.

I was escorted into a bare room with only a table, an American flag, and the United States Army Insignia on the wall. There was also a T.V. and a video tape machine in the room.

The M.P.s on duty in the Presidio sat me down and I waited. After a very slow hour, two aides came in with a balding man in dress uniform. The man had two stars on his uniform. He was a Major General.

"Egan," he said flatly.

"Yes, Sir," I replied. "Formerly of the Eighty Second Airborne."

He shuffled some papers around and smiled a sinister smile. Now there were four people present, but the room seemed too quiet.

He looked at me briefly and stated, "Your status is not "formerly" soldier," he said. "You've still got sixty-two days left of your enlistment."

I was startled. "That could not be, Sir," I said. I produced my Document of Completion of Service-my Discharge papers from my pocket.

"These mean nothing," he said. There was a long pause. "I do not like to have men under my command committing crimes."

He repeated more emphatically, almost yelling, "Committing Crimes!"

"What did I do?" I begged to know.

"You defaced your medals and embarrassed the Commander in Chief!"

I was upset. "That's no crime," I replied.

"You are AWOL, and you owe the Army sixty-two more days." His voice was cold. "I've a mind to court martial you."

"This is insane," I said. I was aghast at his accusation.

"We have a video of you," he said. "What do you have to say for yourself?"

"I know you are a General," I said peevishly. "But why pick on me?"

"It's what you represent," He said with finality. "You are the most decorated Non-Commissioned Officer I've ever come across and when you make a statement people listen. That is not good for the War effort."

"War effort, my ass, Sir," I said. "People are dying over there to protect Shell Oil. It makes me enraged that the Army has become the tool of the corporations."

"Is that what you think?" he said and raised his one eyebrow at me.

"What?" I said. "You didn't get those stars by being naïve, Sir. Can't you hear the giant sucking sound of Wall Street as you defend liberty? I can!"

The look in his eyes became stoney and he spoke very slowly with precision. "You have two choices, Soldier. You can sign this form admitting you committed a crime, or you can go through a Court Martial Hearing. What will it be?"

"If I sign it, what will I get?" I asked.

"A General Discharge," General Broward said. "And the Army forgets about your ass."

"Otherwise," he continued after a pause for effect. "You know what a Court Martial is?"

He had me and he knew it.

"You are a Two Star Son of a Bitch!" I hissed at him.

I didn't even have to consider. I knew that a court martial was messy and I would lose. In the Army it's what they call military justice. You go in guilty and then you must prove your innocence.

I didn't know until this event that oftentimes one's Discharge Papers do not correspond with required days of service. They had me on video and though I hadn't realized it at the time, I was still in the service. According to the General I was not innocent, and I was guilty of everything he said I was. I was not in the mood to carry the General's charade off any longer. I just wanted out.

"Where's the pen?" I asked in a surly voice.

I looked at the form – 1666/DD. My crimes were listed in detail. I sounded like a real bad man.

I signed on the dotted line.

I looked the old bastard in the eye with a sincere wish to wring his fat neck.

He nodded his head and two healthy young MPs escorted me out the door and off the base.

Then I wished I had never heard of Don McKenzie, the protester who had manipulated me and urged me to go with him. I wish I had kept a better tally of enlistment days. Would have, could have, should have. It was done.

I made my way back to #3 Bay Street with a sick feeling. I no sooner collapsed in bed, feeling sorry for myself and wishing I had emigrated to Canada before I was drafted, when the phone rang. It was my friend, Old Joe.

"Where you been, Son?" he questioned. "I've got you a job."

I didn't even ask what the job was. At this point I would have shoveled shit at the back of the governor's Pride Parade if it paid me a few bucks.

"Tell you what," he continued. "Meet me down at the restaurant. We'll have lunch and discuss the job.

"I'll be there," I said. "Noon?"

"A little before, if you can make it."

"You got it," I said as I hung up.

Old Joe had a way of making the sun shine for me so many times, no matter what the weather was.

I had a restless night's sleep. I dreamed of doing serious bodily harm to General A. Broward for the example he had made of me. I could not shake off the anger.

I showered and prepared to walk out the door to meet Joe when the phone rang.

"Hello!" I answered.

"Hey, this is Joe," he said. "You got the keys to the Limo?"

"Yeah, right next to the apartment keys."

"Well, float that boat down to the restaurant. Park right in front." A click and he was gone.

"Okay," I said to myself. "Today we travel by Limo."

In the garage I warmed the motor and thought about the situation. It was a brand new 1970 Lincoln. It still had the dealer tags on it. I hoped my military I.D. was still legal to drive the car.

The car floated on the narrow San Francisco Streets. In five minutes, I was parked in the 'Reserved' spot in front of the restaurant.

As I walked through the door Joe met me.

"We've got to go in back to see Barry," he said. "He's my brother and needs a driver with special skills." Joe winked at me as if I knew what he meant.

I walked with him into the office and then through a door marked "Employees Only." A slim grey-haired man was sitting behind a well-organized desk.

XX

The Job

Joe's brother was obviously a big shot and used to ordering things to be done for his business. His tone reminded me of military orders. I did not ask questions.

"Let's go for a ride," he said.

The Limo plainly belonged to him and I took on the role of Limo Driver and Chauffer.

"Let's go to Sausalito," he said.

I turned the car back to Van Ness Avenue, turned left out on Lombard, over the bridge-and there we were. He directed me to pull up in front of 27 Bay Spring row, a marvelous five-bedroom, four bath, two story unit right on the bay. It had its own private deck.

"You're hired," Barry said. "Can you shoot a gun?"

I said modestly, "I think three years in Nam qualifies me."

"Yes, I believe it would," Barry said with dry humor.

I still did not ask any questions and Barry and Joe told me no lies. It was a job and I needed one.

Barry reached into his pocket, pulled out his wallet and handed me four one hundred-dollar bills. He reached over to me and stuffed them in my shirt pocket.

"A week in advance," he said. "The only drawback to this job is you must be ready to bring the car anytime I need you. Agreed?"

"Agreed!" I answered. Those four bills were heavy incentive.

"The gun and permit will be in your right-hand dresser drawer. Your new license will be there too."

Barry added. "I'd like to see you here at this address at 5:30 a.m."

"Good enough, sir," I said.

Barry looked at Joe and laughed. "You train 'em young, don't you?"

"This one since he was ten years old," Joe said. They laughed together.

"There's a beeper for you in that drawer too," Joe said to me.

I took Joe back into the city and we had lunch at a Chinese joint, the Lotus Blossom Café.

For once I could pick up the check. My wallet felt fat in my hand and in my pocket.

When I returned to #3 Bay Street I found everything right where they said it would be, a nice S & W .357 with holster, a class III license from the DMV with my name on it, and a beeper. My gun permits were inside the holster.

I also found a good-looking blonde making up the bed and changing the towels.

"Excuse me?" I said.

"Oh, Mr. Egan?"

"Yes, that's me," I replied. I felt very uncomfortable to know someone was in my room I didn't know.

"Joe sent me over to tidy up for you," she said. "And anything else you might want."

In my mind I thought, "How subtle Old Joe is."

She stayed the night. Her name was Della.

I was at Barry's front door the next morning at 5:30 sharp. He slipped out the front door as he was putting on his suit jacket. Mrs. Barry, her real name was Conchita, handed him his briefcase.

"Good morning," he said to me with a flat voice. He didn't say another word until we were in front of his restaurant. He smiled and his long thin face drew up into a wrinkled grin, then went solemn again.

"Did you enjoy Della?" he asked.

"Best welcome home present I've had so far," I replied.

"Good. Good," he said and nodded. Everything else there too?"

He smiled again, turned and went into the office.

I knew he had a meeting at noon, then home again by 4:30 p.m. He was a man of meticulous habits.

It was approaching April 1971, before anything changed for me.

Other members of Barry's family started to drift in from the East Coast. They were rude and surly toward me when I was told to transport them here or there. They treated me like a paid slave.

"Hey, you – driver," said one of the loud-mouthed East Coast guys. "Get your ass over to the Four Clovers Bar and pick up Johnny C."

I drove him, but it irritated the hell out of me. I knew something was bound to happen with one of these guys.

One day I had just picked Barry up from his home. He was stepping out of the car in front of his restaurant and a man I recognized as Johnny C had a gun in his hand and was getting out of a separate vehicle.

I didn't trust this guy and thought he was going to shoot Barry. In my military-trained mind I knew how to protect Barry. My gun was tucked into my holster under my uniform coat. Instantly my weapon was in my hand and I had fired three shots at the so-called gentleman across the street before I thought about it.

He went down, swearing at me in Italian.

Barry was next to me and put his hand on my shoulder and called the police with his other hand on his mobile phone.

"Stay still John," he said. "You did the right thing."

The police drove up with guns drawn, ready for battle, but Barry stood up to them and defended me.

"Sorry you were called in," he said to the policemen calmly. "It was a dreadful accident. I will call the mayor and get it straight."

Then he nodded at the police and said very quietly, "Thank you for your quick response."

The man I had shot had been cleaning his gun, waiting to talk to Barry. He still had the gun in his hand, not thinking to put it away, when Barry had stepped from the car.

I was lucky I hadn't killed the man, only grazed his right leg.

The Emergency vehicle arrived in the midst of sirens. The EMTs were very concerned as they drove him away.

I was put on a short leash after that. Barry had to meet with some family members in private, with me not involved. Some of the family wanted my head.

In the end Johnny C admitted he was in the wrong, issues were dropped, and the family relented.

I reviewed in my mind how trouble seemed to follow me like an ill wind. Was I bad luck? "Good Lord," I said to myself, "It's always something."

One night I asked Della, "What's your last name?"

"LaPonte," she said.

"You're Carlo LaPonte's daughter?" I asked.

"Uh, hmm," she replied.

"What are you doing here with me?" I asked.

She was standing at the dresser and she gently traced a pattern on the dresser.

"I'm just keeping an eye on you. And you're the best man I've ever had in bed."

"Oh, my god," I began.

"My daddy says it's alright just as long as I'm having fun." She giggled.

I knew then I was hip deep in trouble once again, and all I had wanted was a job.

About a month after the shooting incident Barry decided he'd take me to the fancy restaurant Top of the Mark, to thank me for my act of protection.

XXI

Chauffer

It was six o'clock in the evening. In front of Barry's restaurant, I picked up Barry, Joe, Conchita and Della, plus a woman I did not know.

We had a table reserved at the Top of the Mark. I had changed into a regular suit rather than my Chauffer's uniform, but I still packed the .357 tucked under my left arm and invisible.

The other woman with us was Joe's daughter, Leah. She had been Joe's companion ever since his wife died three years before. Leah was a very classy lady.

She was five foot eight inches tall, with a beautiful figure and intelligent, piercing eyes. You could see that wherever she went, she was the boss.

Her hair was dark black, and she did not take second place to any other lady in the room.

Joe turned toward me but addressed this elegant woman.

"Leah, I'd like you to meet John Egan," Joe said. "He's Barry's driver."

She looked at me with those eyes and deep down into my soul. She smiled.

My reaction was that I hoped she liked what she saw.

Then Leah looked toward Della with a sly cat-like look in her eyes and said, "Della."

Della replied with a hidden meaning just as strongly, "Leah."

"Now you girls get along," Joe interjected. "We're here to offer Mr. Egan a little something for his quick thinking and acting, not to air your past grievances."

"Uh oh," I thought to myself.

Dinner was ordered. I asked for one Manhattan. I thought that one was safe since I was the driver.

The man playing the piano introduced himself as Ed Bingham. Leah said he was a big shot in the Bay Area music business.

Joe leaned toward me and said, "You play, don't you Johnny?"

"Yeah," I replied. "I like to write my own songs."

Joe smiled and said, "We ought to hear some of them. Why don't you go over there and play one for us?"

"Oh, Joe," I smiled back at him. "You don't go stealing the show when some other guy is playing. It's just not done."

"Bet the man would step aside for $100 bill," said Barry. "I'd like to hear you."

So, it came to pass, as the saying goes, that Mr. Bingham introduced me to the restaurant crowd, and I got up and played a song.

Instead of one of my own I played the new John Lennon song I liked very much called "Imagine." When I was done, I got a standing ovation, right there in the restaurant.

Ed Bingham said to me, "Hey Buddy, you are good! You need to come down to our studio and let Leo record you." He handed me his card.

When I sat back down Leah put her hand on my arm and said, "John, you were magnificent."

At the end of the evening I dropped Barry and Conchita at their front door. Leah took Joe home in her car but not before an exchange of bitchy looks between her and Della.

Della and I went back to #3 Bay St.

I asked Della, "What's up between you and Leah?"

"Oh," Della moaned. "It goes back to schoolgirl stuff. I just can't stand the way she acts so superior and everything. I guess we should bury the hatchet." She paused, "Just as long as it's in her head."

I backed away from any more questions about that rivalry.

It had been a long day. The bed was soft and so was Della. My eyes closed on their own and for a change I didn't awaken to dreams of gunfire.

It was Friday, my day off. I decided to go down to Golden State Studios and take Mr. Bingham up on his offer.

When I found the place, I was amazed to find it was built on a hill just around the corner from Broadway and Golden Gate Ave. The building was huge. There was no receptionist., just a very busy secretary who asked me who I was looking for. Her desk was at the bottom of a long cement stairway that went to the second floor.

"Mr. Bingham, please," I said.

She shouted over her shoulder, "Hey Ed — there's someone here to see you."

I heard his voice from upstairs saying something unintelligible. She smiled at me and said, "Sit down and he'll get to you in a bit."

Ed came wandering down the stairway with his half glasses pushed up over his balding head. When he saw me sitting there a big grin came over his face and he greeted me.

"Mr. Egan!"

"Mr. Bingham." I answered formally.

"Glad you could find the time to come and see me," he said. "Let me introduce you to the owner of this place, Mr. Leo Degar Kulke. Come on upstairs."

I trudged up the stairs behind Ed, to find another balding man who looked to be in his fifties. His eyes were heavy with dark circles under them. Hanging from his lips was a large cigar, and when he reached out to shake my hand his eyes viewed me with a guarded and cynical look.

"What can I do for you, Mr. Egan?" he asked.

"I don't know," I replied. "I came down because Ed said I should."

Ed interrupted just then and said, "You need to hear this guy. I think he could be our next money maker."

"Okay," said Leo. "Let's go down to the piano and you play everything you've got for me. I'll get Vance to record it."

We all scurried downstairs to the studio booth where I met Vance Frost. Vance was clearly the hippie in residence and the recording engineer. He sat me down at the huge grand piano that was in the middle of the studio.

I had never recorded in a studio before and I knew I had a lot of bad habits. Vance saw them all and knew how to get a good sound out of me no matter what.

Leo and Ed watched from the recording booth. Leo said again into the microphone, "Play me everything you've got, John. I'll stop you when I hear something I can use."

I played and sang. I felt I was rusty and nervous, but I was part way through one of the last songs I'd written before I'd gone to Nam.

Leo clicked on the microphone and said, "That one. Start again from the beginning. Give it your soul."

When I finished the song he said to Vance, "Take."

He invited me into the booth and Vance played it back for us. I sounded better than I could ever remember sounding.

"I've got a group coming in from Canada," said Leo. "They're looking for a single. I think this one is it."

"What's the name of the group?" I asked.

"Silverhill," said Leo. "A fine group of boys."

I looked up at the wall where four golden records were hung. I could see they were from the fifties by the same artist.

"That was the guy who did "Alley Oop," I said. I was impressed.

Pamela, the secretary, typed up a contract between Degar Publishing ASCAP and myself, giving me five cents royalty for every record that would sell.

I pointed out the paltry sum with a question on my face.

"That's standard for first time song writers," Leo said. "This will make us both some money."

He smiled and stuffed a hundred-dollar bill in my pocket.

"Call it an advance on royalties," he said.

The Silverhill Boys' session was immaculate; they had three-part harmony on the hook line, and then they moved the song like a slick snake through grass. I almost didn't recognize my own music.

Della came to that session with me.

"So how long you gonna keep working as Barry's driver?" she asked.

"Ah, this is just a side-line, Honey." I believed my own words. "What money would I eat on with this gig?"

She laughed. It was plain she was nervous about losing me.

"Hey, you're my girl until you don't want to be anymore," I reassured her.

"I think I love you," she muttered. I almost didn't hear her.

"I think I love you too," I said as I reached out and rubbed her knee.

She beamed at me and I noticed the spring in her step the rest of the day.

It took three weeks to complete the Silverhill album. Then the group was back on the road to Canada. Stew, the lead guitarist, had me play some harmony leads with him and the guys all agreed it was ready for market. Leo was shopping around to various record labels to see if anyone would bite.

That's when it felt like lightning struck.

XXII

CBS Records

It was about three o'clock in the afternoon and I was driving Barry. My beeper went off just as I dropped Barry off at home. Who could be calling me now? I had the mobile phone in the car, so I dialed the number calling me. A neat, clean secretarial voice answered, saying "CBS Records."

"Hi, "I said. "My name us Johnny Egan and I'm returning a phone call from this number."

"Oh, yes, Mr. Egan," she said. I could have sworn she was chewing bubble gum. "George has been trying to get hold of you. Let me transfer you to him."

There was a short beep and a voice with a New York accent answered.

"Johnny!" he said. I've been trying to get hold of you. We listened to the Silverhill album and we have decided to pass on it, but Clive is interested in you. Could you come down to our office and talk?"

"Me?" I questioned. "I'm just the song writer."

"Yes, indeed," he replied. "There's a big market now for singer songwriters...are you interested?"

"I could be there this afternoon. Where are you located?"

"Let's make it for tomorrow about ten," George said. "The big guy is coming in from New York tonight and wants to meet you."

"I'm still on call in the morning at ten," I said. "But I can slip out of work for a little while. Where's your office?"

"The Cannery, at the end of Columbus," he said. "At ten. 'Bye."

There was a click, and the secretary came back on.

"Are you there?" she asked.

"Yeah," I answered.

"Things move fast around here," she said. "My name is Karen Gilbert, room 101 at the Cannery. Ten o'clock then?"

"I'll be there with bells on," I said.

The next morning, I dropped Barry off at the restaurant then went to the market to pick up Conchita, then to find a place to park the Limousine.

By ten I was at the Cannery Office Building knocking on the door of 101.

I walked down a hallway glittering with CBS Record labels - Gold and Platinum records, huge photos of past artists, and at the end of the hall the cutest secretary sitting behind a gigantic desk.

"Hello," I said. "I'm Johnny Egan."

"Hi, I'm Karen Gilbert," she smiled. "George will be out shortly."

The door to her left had a sign that read, A & R, with George L. Daly in big letters beneath. The glass window of the door was opaque and sparkly.

I felt like I had dropped into a pawn broker's dream.

Suddenly the door flew open and there stood George L. Daly. He was six foot one, looked like he hadn't shaved in at least three days. He wore grey slacks and a tweed jacket with leather pads at the elbows. Under the jacket he wore a white T shirt. On his feet were Birkenstock sandals with no socks. He had one thick long eyebrow extending over both his dark brown eyes.

He seemed in a hurry as he said to Karen Gilbert, "Where's that Egan character?"

Karen just pointed at me.

"Mr. Egan," he said in a clipped New York accent, "Let's talk."

He ushered me into his office with a large hand on my shoulder.

"We were listening to the Silverhill album," he said. "That single is great!"

"We passed on the group," he continued. They don't seem to fit our current push model, but you! You fit!"

"What are you asking from me?" I queried.

"Do you want to be a CBS recording artist?" he said.

"I assume there's more to it than signing on the dotted line," I replied. I was trying to appear not so naïve, but I had no idea of the implications.

"Yeah," George Daly said. "First we have to do a demo and then you gotta do an audition. But you're up for that?"

I felt like I was being hustled and there was one more fact or two I could not see behind his offer.

"I'm going to book you a session over at Heider's," George said. "We'll get it done."

We exchanged small talk for a short while then he was plainly impatient and ready to go. He scooted me out to Secretary Karen to "make arrangements."

"What's George Daly in such a hurry for?" I asked Karen.

"Don't you know?" she said.

"No, I haven't got a clue," I responded.

"The big guy is coming to town - Clive Davis, and he hasn't got all the things done that he needs to get done."

"Ha!" I exclaimed. "Lazy Bones Parker."

"Excuse me?" she said.

"That's a joke we had in the military about a corporal named Parker who was always so lazy he was getting caught with things unfinished. He was called Duty Shy by his Sergeant."

"How quaint," Karen replied, lifting her eyebrow in a saucy way. "I'll give you a call when your demo time is booked."

By the time I got back to where the Limousine was parked the mobile phone was ringing off the hook. It was Della.

"What's up, Honey?" I answered.

"There are two men here looking for you," she said.

At first, I was apprehensive, remembering the FBI men. Then she added, one is black and the other fellow looks Jewish.

My heart leaped for joy. It was Willie T. Devoy and Big Dick Zieback! They made it home!

"Tell them I'll be home directly."

As I hung up I yelled, "Wahoo! They survived! They fucking survived!"

I was so glad I almost ran the red light at Van Ness.

When I pulled up at #3 Bay Street Willie T and Big Dick were out on the steps drinking some of that fine Italian coffee Della was famous for.

"You done real good, Sarge," Willie T. said.

"We thought you was a goner when you got that head wound."

"So did I," I replied. "But the wonders of medical science," I explained. "The doctors said it looked a lot worse than it was."

"So what happened back then when I got injured?" I asked.

"There was a pack of VC rats." Big Dick explained. "They were pulling two wheeled wagons so we thought they were civilians. We didn't recognize them until they were on top of us."

"There was a shot, and you went down, then all hell broke loose. Bullets were flying all around. We returned fire but we were pinned down until an ARVN unit came to our rescue. Us two and Gary are the sole survivors of our platoon."

"Have you ever heard from Gary?" I asked.

Willie T. answered. "Last I heard, they were trying new medicine on him and the other Clap victims down there. He wrote that most days he doesn't even know he's infected."

I sighed, "That's a relief to know."

"What about you?" asked Big Dick. "Looks like you've done pretty good out of all this."

"It's up in the air right now," I answered. "My old childhood friend Joe, you know, the old guy I told you kept me out of trouble when I was a kid, he got me a job and this apartment, but it all feels temporary. For now it's good."

"What about your woman?" Big Dick asked. "She seems mighty fine."

"Oh, that's Della LaPonte," I said. "She's keeping an eye on me."

"Damned fine eye," Big Dick chuckled under his breath.

"She's a free spirit," I laughed.

It felt good to be together. It had been a long time since we could bullshit freely with each other.

"Say," I asked. "What ever happened to that Marine, Captain Granger after his woman was killed?"

Both men's faces dropped.

"He committed suicide," Willie T. said. "He was so upset about losing his woman. He jumped out of an airplane just before they reached Nha Trang."

"I wondered about him," I said. "He was in a bad way."

"Hey," Willie T. said with more enthusiasm in his voice. "Looks like you're going to be a star. Are you gonna have time for your old war buddies now?"

"That star business can kiss my ass," I replied. "You two and I have chewed too much of the same dirt to let that be water under the bridge.

Both Willie T. and Big Dick smiled.

"You got a place to stay yet?" I asked.

"Yeah, we've got a room down in the Tenderloin till we get our feet under us."

"Where?" I asked.

"The old Jefferson Hotel," said Big Dick. "The beds are semi clean."

"You know you can bunk here, if Della doesn't mind," I offered.

"Nah," they said in unison. "We can at least take advantage of the hookers down there."

"Let me drive you to the hotel at least," I insisted.

"You got it," Willie T. said. "They gonna like us when they see that Limousine."

They tumbled into the Limo and I took them downtown.

"You know I stayed down here when I first got back from Nam," I said. "It is pretty much a hole."

"Yeah, it is," said Big Dick. "But it's what we could afford."

"I told you that you could bunk with me till you get situated," I said.

"Thanks, but we gotta live our own adventure here, Sarge," Willie T. responded. "We'll be up to bug you often enough."

I shook my head. Then it was a ten-minute drive to the rundown Tenderloin of San Francisco, filled with gangs and heroin addicts. The hookers gathered around the Limousine as I parked it. They licked their lips and wiggled, showing off their bodily curves.

"You sure about hangin' in this neighborhood?" I asked my two buddies.

"It's no worse than downtown Saigon," said Big Dick. "We survived that, and I think we'll survive this."

I drove around the block and went past a new bar. The sign was hand-painted and read, "Ram's Head Tavern." As I moved past slowly two men appeared in the street, fighting. One of them took a straight razor out of his pocket and cut the other man's throat.

The police showed up and stopped all the traffic. They arrested the man with the razor, while the other one lay on the pavement choking for dear life.

I rolled down the car window and asked, "Officer, aren't you going to see to that man's injuries?"

He scowled at me and said, "Damned fags! He cut the man's throat and totally missed the carotids. Can't even do that right!"

He turned his back to me as the EMTs showed up to take care of the injured man.

Then I knew that the world was just as disgusting here in the city as it was in Viet Nam. In fact – in Asia they seemed more honest about their prejudices and hatreds. I wondered again what the world had become.

XXIII

The Audition

Two weeks later I met with George Daly at the Heiders' Studio down on Broadway. He had hired four other musicians to back me up to make a Demo. I felt humble in their presence because they were very well known, pretty big-time guys. Harvey Brooks on bass guitar, George Chenkas on drums, Pete Weir on guitar, and Leon Russell on piano.

The session went great. We recorded three tunes that were class A rock 'n roll. Leon sort of ran the thing, saying to me, "Johnny, just relax. It'll be really great," and it was. They scheduled an audition for the big wigs for the very next week.

The day of the audition I was nervous. It meant a lot to get a contract with CBS Records. I arrived early at Heiders' again. They wheeled out the grand piano for me to play.

Six men that looked more suited for working at a bank, sat in the audience. I went into the show as planned and sang and played my three tunes.

I had noticed five or six other shadowy figures in the recording booth, one I recognized as Phoebe Snow. I had always loved her music.

When it was over all the people left quietly without applause. I thought I had dumped the audition and was feeling low. Then Phoebe Snow came bouncing out of the recording booth. She tweaked my ear and kissed me gently on the cheek.

She said, "You were great, Johnny!"

Then she added with a smile, "Don't worry about the stuffed shirts. They did the same to me!"

She made me feel much better.

George Daly and Leon Russell were still in the booth. They had recorded me and when they came out, they said the playback didn't sound half bad.

"I think you made it," said Leon. "Congratulations."

I stumbled out of the studio in shock. An old Army guy like myself suddenly getting a chance at the big time.

I started thinking. I could not keep the chauffer's job. I would not have #3 Bay Street to live in and more important, I would no longer have Della.

Things were moving way too fast and I needed to talk to some people.

At home Della was at the kitchen table in a sulk.

"You heard?" I asked.

"Yeah, I heard," she said. "Congratulations," she added in a soft voice.

"If the record goes, I'll be on the road a lot. Are you okay with that?"

"I suppose you're going to throw me away like so much trash," she said. She was almost crying.

"No, Baby. I'm not," I told her. "You are the one thing in this last year that has kept me sane. I want you to stay by my side forever."

"Is that a proposal I hear coming?" she said. She turned her face to me, and her eyes were shining hopefully.

"I guess it is," I said. "Will you come with me?"

"You betcha, Mister!" she said. She jumped up and hugged me.

In the end I had to square it all with Barry and old Joe. Most of all I had to face Carlo La Ponte, Della's father.

Della stood beside me as I faced Mr. La Ponte. His response to me was, "So you want to take my little girl on a hayride, huh?"

"Yes, sir. I do," I said, looking him straight in the eye.

He paused and looked at Della.

"Whatever my little girl wants," he said. Then he added, "Don't beat her more than twice a week." He laughed.

It was a crazy time in my life. Johnny Egan, soldier, chauffer, and now a Rock Star. Ain't America wonderful?

It was agreed that Della would keep #3 Bay Street to live in and I would pay a modest rent to Barry for the place.

Barry told me, "Keep this chauffer job till you have to go on the road. Then I'll hire a substitute driver for when you do." That sounded reasonable to me.

XIV

No Soft Landing

It's been decades now since the bright young kid known as Johnny Egan looked in the mirror as a Rock Star. The big CBS record contract was short-lived. I had been hopeful and excited when CBS handed me a contract, but I was naïve. For a short space of eight months I believed all my dreams of becoming a Star were coming through. I had no clue that I should have had a lawyer with me at the contract signing.

When those eight months were up, I was invited to a meeting with the CEO of the record company. He said the music market had changed and that the company could no longer "sell" me. Therefore it was no longer advantageous to continue our relationship.

I was confused, devastated and angry. I had a high sense of failure. Their tactic was to send me a bill through CBS's inhouse publishing. This was for my having used their studio time and tour support to the tune of $38,922 - a small fortune in 1971.

Much later I learned that the contract should have had four sections. In the music business a contract should have a white page outlining an initial agreement between two parties. A yellow page showing the share of costs where the company fronts you an amount - for me that was about $20,000, and that you agree to pay it back. The pink page lists the musician's responsibilities. The blue page of the contract is actually what the rights of the musician are. That page was missing from my contract. The other three pages were originally presented to me as though they were a complete contract, but that fourth page was left out deliberately.

Looking back I suspected the agency had a plan to let me go in a short time. I had written and recorded ten songs in their studio which was to become an album. They now owned the songs, I had no rights to my own music, and I was let go before an album could be completed and released.

At the same time I was let go I heard that they wanted James Taylor to join CBS, but he was out of commission for a time and was in rehab. When he had become rehabilitated, they offered him a contract. I was grateful when I learned from other musicians that he declined the offer from CBS and opted for a contract with Apple Records.

CBS had several other rising musicians in their sites at the same time as me, and I learned it was their practice to have four or five rising stars on their payroll. CBS could invest $30,000 in each of those musicians and let go whomever they decided not to continue to give backing to. This practice was known as "Long Arming."

I confided my distress to my friend Henry, who was in the music business.

"You hang on, Johnny," he said when I told him about the horrendous bill I had been handed.

"I have a music lawyer friend who owes me a favor. I think he can fix things."

I sat in Henry's office when he called his lawyer friend, Joe, and told him the situation.

Henry sent me off to Joe's office. He was a hard-faced man, knew his business and knew exactly what to do. In my hearing he called someone I didn't know and said, "Do you want to buy one of Johnny's songs and a section of two others of his songs?"

Lawyer Joe negotiated the cost of the sale and said, "It's $50,000. Is it a deal?"

The person on the other end of the line agreed. Lawyer Joe made and completed arrangements for the unknown buyer to pay the bill through CBS's inhouse publishing.

The whole deal procedure took all of twenty minutes.

As Lawyer Joe turned his attention back to me, he said, "Son, this is hard ball we play here. If you're not willing to play hard ball I don't want you to ever darken my door again. Now get out!"

I learned much later in the 1980's that CBS had sold all ten of my songs to a Japanese company called Skippio Records. I had no rights of recovery from that company.

After the bill was settled that I had owed to CBS I was invited to join some high school buddies who had gone professional and formed a band. We traveled to various gigs for a couple of years, and I lived with Della at Bay Street when not on the road. I continued to play guitar and piano and sing solo. On my own time I continued to write music but did not perform any of my original works. Within four years we signed with ABC Records. We became the opening band for several well-known singers.

Even though we were often on the road, Della and I had begun a family. In 1975 we had a baby girl and thoughts began to rise in my mind that my small family needed more stability.

With ABC Records we were assigned to go on tour with Roy Orbison, and for two years we traveled as far north as Canada and as far south as Baton Rouge. I often opened as lead guitarist.

I made hundreds of thousands of dollars from 1974 through 1978. By then I was realizing that for me the fun had gone out of the Rock Star status. The clincher was that the United States and Canada income taxes on us were so steep that when both countries had been paid, we hardly had enough to live on. Our second child was born in 1977, and I felt the real need to have a steady income. Those little ones needed shirts, shoes, food and shelter when they needed it – not when I might have the money.

I returned to school and earned a Ba in Health Services and for thirty years have rendered care giving to people in need. I had always taken interest in health issues and the work satisfied my need to give back services similar to what I had been given when I had been injured.

XXV

Reflections

There is always music in my background, and I've been part of several bands that played gigs on the North Coast, but only weekends. And I've made a couple of albums of listening music available on the internet, but which bring me no income.

The only thing I kept from the old days is Della. She bore me two fine children and looks as good to me today as when I first met her.

Barry and Joe have since passed away and rarely do I hear from Big Dick or Willie T.

My daughter has borne three children, making me a grandfather. My son is a hell raiser, which I believe he comes by naturally from his old man. He tumbled back into my life last week from one of his many journeys. He came to confide in me something new in his life. His girlfriend announced to him that he was becoming a father.

The look in his eyes of desperation and caring reminded me of ages ago when Della gave me the news that I would be a father. My son has no steady job, and the reality has hit him that a child needs things that only stability and responsibility can give.

Then I saw the circle of life had made a full turn as my son found his identity as a father.

"Congratulations, Son." I smiled much as my father might have done. "Now I wish you good luck with the newness of life coming to you."

When I reflect on my life I am still dissatisfied and distressed with how my War Service turned out. I feel my government has cheated me. I knew my father had served in a just war that liberated the world from dominance by evil forces. He had gained skill in his several years as a military mechanic which gave him a well-paid profession. I on the other hand, had several scars and a brain injury that triggered epilepsy. The meds I've taken are expensive and poisonous to my system and I've had no Veteran's benefits to assist me because I had inadvertently discarded them by protesting the Viet Nam War, a war that most Americans decry as one of our worst mistakes.

My bitterness is assuaged only by the hope that younger Veterans of more modern wars and police actions will have the benefits they deserve, that our government will care for its veterans as has been promised. But for me it is clear that not only the saying "War is hell," is true but that it is an awful reality that continues with me until today.

www.ingramcontent.com/pod-product-compliance
Lightning Source LLC
Chambersburg PA
CBHW060149130626
46556CB00006B/2566